The Adventures Of

Crimson And The Guardian

The Adventures Of
Crimson And The Guardian

*A Medieval Story of an Orphan Explorer
and a Unicorn Legend*

Karen Cossey

Paperback and Kindle Edition Published 2017
Publisher: Stolen Moments
An Imprint of Tui Valley Books Limited
ISBN: 978-0-473-38119-6
Kindle version: ISBN: 978-0-473-35971-3

Map Illustration by: Renflowergraphx

Publisher's Note:

Find Karen's Other Books here
www.karencossey.com
Follow Karen on Facebook here:
www.facebook.com/KarenCosseyAuthor
or Instagram here:
www.instagram.com/karencosseywriter/
or Pinterest here:
https://www.pinterest.nz/karencosseyauthor/

Dedication

This book is dedicated to my family: Peter, Daniel and Amy,
and my 'international sons': Thiago and Johannes.
You are all wonderful people whom I treasure greatly.

𝔉ree 𝔅ook:

The Crime Stopper Kids Mysteries Prequel

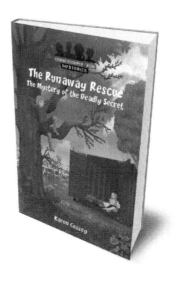

The Runaway Rescue
The Mystery of the Deadly Secret
For 9-13-year-olds

When Cole and Poet's father is killed, they are left with no one to take care of them. Fearing separation by Social Services, a desperate eleven-year-old Cole runs away with his seven-year old sister Lauren. With nowhere to turn they take a chance on a stranger's help, but when danger comes knocking at the stranger's door, Cole wonders if he'll ever be safe again. How far will he have to run this time to protect himself and Lauren?

**Receive the whole story FOR FREE
when you sign up to Karen's newsletter at:
www.KarenCossey.com/Newsletter/**

Table of Contents

KNOWN WORLD

NAWARA SEA

HUNTERS BAY

ROWANDALE PROVINCE

LORD LINCOLN'S CASTLE

GOLDEN IMRYLL WOODLANDS
(THE ELVES FOREST)

GREENFELL PROVINCE

MILONDERLAND PROVINCE

LORD YEARBURY'S CASTLE

OAKENFURY WOODS
(THE DWARF FOREST)

LORD MONTEITH'S CASTLE

LORD GALVIN'S CASTLE

GRINLINTON PROVINCE

LORD ALEXANDER'S CASTLE

LORD HUDSON'S CASTLE

LLODORNEY PROVINCE

POEMDASH POCKET WOODS
(THE PIXIE FOREST)

MASTER ASHTON'S HOME

HORUNDALE PROVINCE

BLACK SWALLOW WOODLAND

Chapter 1. The River Monster

"Where are the pixies hiding?" I asked myself as I walked through Pixie Forest. Wouldn't it be great to see one? 'Little People,' they were called, and they were known for their dancing and playful ways. If they liked you it was said they could bring you a blessing. They loved exploring—maybe they could take me with them so I could run away.

Before my father had died, I often rode the horses he trained, but now I had to work as Master Ashton's kitchen maid with just my feet to carry me to see my sister, Liliana. She was the Cook's assistant at Lord Hudson's castle, and even had a room to herself because she was so helpful and well-liked. I was a troublemaker—that's what the cook had told me this morning when I'd dropped the oatmeal all over the floor. She'd yelled at me to clear off and not come back until nighttime, so I'd escaped before she changed her mind. I

1

was going to make the most of a day off. Running away with the pixies might not work out, but at least I could see Liliana. Perhaps there would be something nice to eat in her kitchen—that thought made me smile. Maybe I'd look for the pixies another day.

That's when I saw something unexpected lying on the path: a skillfully woven grey-green cloak. I picked it up and felt how soft it was, like the fine mist of the early morning fog on my face, waiting to wrap itself around me. I glanced over my shoulder, looking for the owner. No one was about, so I put it on, unable to resist the temptation to be enveloped in something so smooth. As I closed the clasp around my neck, I heard a firm voice behind me.

"That's it then. You're the one."

I spun around in time to see a white unicorn step out from behind a tree!

I stared at her, not believing what my eyes were showing me. Then, to my amazement, her mouth started moving and words came out!

"It's about time you turned up. I've been waiting for someone to come along and try on the cloak. All I've seen go past the last couple of days are thieving pixies who want to make it into blankets."

My knees went weak and I sat down hard on the ground, staring at the unicorn. A talking unicorn! I'd heard rumors that there were a few unicorns left in the land, but I'd always believed unicorns were only a legend. Yet here was one right in front of me—and it could talk!

"Who are you?" I asked with a tremble in my voice.

"I'm Crimson," she said. "I watch over Sir Ivor."

I recognized the name. Sir Ivor was a national hero. He'd slain dragons, scared all the witches from the kingdom, and defeated the giant trolls single-handedly. Was the cloak his?

3

"I'm . . . I'm sorry. Where is he? I wasn't stealing his cloak. I only meant to try it on for a minute. I'll put it back here for him," I babbled as I yanked at the clasp, trying to open it.

It stayed shut, like the mouth of a young child refusing to eat his vegetables.

"He's not coming back," Crimson said. "He left the cloak for me to give to his successor. That's you. I hope you didn't have any other major life plans. It is a full-time job being a heroine." She smiled at me.

I felt like a cat thrown in a deep river.

"I'm no heroine. I'm just an ordinary kitchen maid on my way to visit my sister at Lord Hudson's castle. Please, just take the cloak and give it back to Lord Ivor," I said as I tugged at the clasp.

"Lord Ivor's retired and gone back to his family across the sea. Now, I need you to stop trying to remove the cloak and come with me. There's a commotion going on at the castle. You need to help sort it out before your sister gets hurt. Climb on my back."

She stared at me and I felt strange, as if I had to do what she said. Before I knew what had happened I was in the saddle she was wearing and galloping towards the castle.

As we approached, I saw a blood-chilling sight: a gigantic river monster in the castle's moat! It looked fierce, like a colossal red snake with orange and black stripes all over its body. Its eyes were like blazing fire, and its fangs pointed like daggers. Water shook off its body as it waved backwards and forwards, trying to reach the windows near the top of the castle's tower. It would only be a few more minutes before it got high enough to slither through them. I could hear terrified screaming coming from inside. I was paralyzed with fear myself as I sat, motionless, on Crimson's back.

"Off you go then," Crimson said, nodding her head in the direction of the monstrous creature.

"Wha . . . wha . . . what?" I stammered.

"Reach inside the cloak. There is a pocket, and inside the pocket is the dragon dagger. It's magic—it kills dragons and river monsters instantly. Once you stab him with it, he'll just . . . poof . . . dissolve away."

"Once I do what?" I forced the panic out of my voice.

"Once you stab him," she said.

"I can't do that. He'll eat me before I get close." I wanted to shout, but I was so scared of the river monster I only managed a hiss.

"Pull the hood of the cloak over your head and you'll be invisible. But be very quiet—he can still hear you. Do it now. He's almost in the tower."

Some kind of power emanated from Crimson and I stopped trembling as I felt a surge of strength and bravery rise up inside me. I tried to fight it off with the last dregs of common sense I possessed, but the strange feeling overwhelmed my terror.

6

My hand betrayed me by reaching up and pulling on the hood, and I vanished! I couldn't see my hands or feet or any other part of myself, nor could I see the cloak. For a brief moment I forgot the river monster and wondered if I was still alive—does a person still exist if they totally disappear?

The roar of monster dragged my attention back and that invading sense of courage which had now reached my head yanked me into action.

I climbed down from Crimson's back and ran nearer to the moat. The monster was stretching up from the other side, about to go through the tower window. He was even more terrifying up close, with saliva drooling from his mouth and an overpowering stench. His skin was made of knife-edged scales. Would I have the strength to push the dagger through them? He was on the opposite side of the moat—how was I to reach him?

I kept running closer but my foot caught on the bottom of the cloak and the traitorous clasp chose that precise moment to come undone! The cloak fell completely off me and I could see myself again. Which meant the river monster could too!

He whirled around and bent his head down toward me, crossing the water. I clutched the dagger with two hands above my head and shut my eyes. His mouth was coming towards me—I knew because I was getting covered in his saliva. Pure fear raced through me. I was about to become his snack. What good could the small blade I held overhead do against the ravenous mouth descending upon me?

But the knife was was the only hope I had, so I jabbed it upwards and felt it connect with the soft tissue inside the monster's mouth. A force like a hurricane knocked me off my feet as the river monster gave a loud, piercing scream . . . and dissolved into nothing. Nothing, that is, except some repulsive, sticky, smelly ooze, which engulfed me.

Crimson was right there beside me.

She smiled as she spoke. "Well, at least you didn't get any monster muck on the cloak."

I wondered if Crimson would disappear if I stabbed her with the dagger.

"Pick up the cloak and climb on my back. It's best to keep you a secret for a while yet. Let's get out of here before someone recognizes you."

I could hear cheers and shouts coming from the castle, so I did as Crimson asked and we galloped back into the forest.

It took a while for me to calm down and wash in the river near where I had met Crimson. She told me to go and visit my sister Liliana, but not to mention anything about the river monster.

When I reached Liliana, she was full of news about the river monster's defeat, saying some people thought they'd seen a child—and even a unicorn!

"Sounds astonishing!" I said with meaning, almost not

believing it had happened. Sitting in the kitchen, eating warm bread, it all seemed like a crazy nightmare. Still, I did as Crimson said and as I left I told Liliana I wouldn't be able to visit for a few months.

I tried to avoid Pixie Forest on the way back, but Crimson found me, just as she said she would. She gave me a kind smile, but this made my urge to run away even stronger.

"Don't run, child," she said in a soothing tone. "You were very brave today. I can tell you are ready for adventure. Sorry for throwing you in the deep end like that, but someone had to do something. It was a bit of a calamity don't you think?"

I pushed down my impulse to rant and rave at her, only because I wanted to hear if she had anything else to say about my being ready for adventure. I still believed she might just disappear any second like some strange dream, and if she had something to say first, I wanted to hear it.

"I think you're ready to give up working in the kitchens and come along with me," she said. "I'll teach you everything you need to know about the cloak. If you come along you'll have the adventures you've always dreamed about."

"I'm not brave enough for adventures," I said. "I was terrified today. It was you and your magic that made me do it."

"True courage comes from acting even when you are scared. You are brave. You just don't believe it. That courage you felt came from within you. I can't put courage inside someone, I can only uncover it."

She looked at me and I knew it was my chance to say no. But I knew I wanted to stay with her and see what the adventures would be. I'd survived the river monster—surely they couldn't be that bad. And anything had to be better than working in Master Ashton's kitchen.

"I'd need to tell Master Ashton I'm leaving," I said.

"We'll do that now. Don't worry. I know your master, and he'll be happy to leave you in my care once I talk with him."

This surprised me and I stared at the ground for a long time, thinking it through. Finally, I lifted my eyes and met hers.

"All right, I'll come along."

Chapter 2. The Jogotchies

The blackness of the night surrendered to the dawn colors as daylight approached. It had been only a few days since we'd said goodbye to a very surprised Master Ashton. He had been concerned that it wasn't safe for young girls to travel alone around the countryside. At his suggestion, I happily agreed to dress as a boy—I preferred trousers to skirts any day.

Crimson gave me the name Malin, which I think was her attempt at a joke. It means Little Warrior, and while I may have been little, I didn't feel much like a warrior. I preferred my own name, Kinsey, which means Royal Victory. I knew it was an oversized name for a kitchen maid, but it always made me smile to think of my parents giving it to me. They must have been dreamers, like me.

Master Ashton also made Crimson promise to bring me back for a visit in a few months, which I looked forward to now I was waking up on the cold hard ground every morning. No more would I complain about my bed of hay at Master Ashton's!

I had no idea where we were, or where we were headed. I sat up and looked for Crimson. Where was she?

I needn't have worried—she was never far away.

"Good morning, Strong Knight of the Kingdom," she said as she stepped into the clearing.

"Don't you mean Peasant from Nowhere?" I groaned. "And I'm a hungry one at that!"

"Look in my saddlebag," she said.

I'd been astonished to find her wearing a saddle. She said it helped her riders, especially Sir Ivor, but she refused to wear a bit and bridle—she was under no one's control. She'd told me to ride like the pixie rogues, with my hands tangled in her mane. I was glad for the saddle, even though my father had taught me to ride bareback. A saddle was easier for long distances at a canter, as we'd been doing the last two days.

I was especially glad for the saddlebag when I reached inside and found an apple pie, still warm. I yanked it out and started gobbling it down.

"Where did you get this?" I asked between mouthfuls.

"From the Castle of Llodorney. It's three miles up the road. The cook's been up all night getting ready for today's banquet."

"Llodorney Castle!" I was surprised. "That's a long way from home. I knew you were moving quickly, but I didn't realise we'd covered so much ground. Do you always travel so fast?"

"Only if there's an urgent need that justifies it."

I stopped eating to digest this information.

"What's the urgent need?" Butterflies started to fight with the pie in my stomach.

"Oh, nothing to worry about. Just a band of jogotchies looking to disrupt Lord Alexander's birthday celebrations. They're a couple of hours away, on the other side of the castle."

"A band of jogotchies!"

I had only ever seen one jogotchy. It had it attacked Master Ashton's horses, dragging one away and devouring it. It had taken Father and Master Ashton three days to track the jogotchy down and kill it. Jogotchies were large creatures, with bodies like apes, four-eyed heads shaped like a wild pig, and mouths filled with three rows of teeth. Mind-hammeringly hideous. They hated water and couldn't run fast, but they were strong and knew how to hide.

"How many is that. . .two, three? Maybe four?" I trembled as the pie in my stomach fought back against the butterflies. I wished I'd taken smaller mouthfuls.

"Oh, just a few, really." She paused and squirmed. "Ten, to be precise. Now don't look so scared. I'd be more worried about the cook if he finds out you ate one of his pies."

The rest of the pie fell to the ground.

"Right, if you're all finished, we'd better be going. Climb up."

A few hours later I was up a tree on a hillside, watching a terror-house of trouble in the form of ten jogotchies passing on the road below. They were speaking to each other in a strange language, and seemed to be plotting something. I had always thought they roamed around by themselves, so looking at ten together sent a chill down my spine.

"What's your plan?" I whispered to Crimson, as I climbed down from the tree.

"Not too sure. Do you have an idea?" she asked. She must have noticed the look on my face because she added, "Calm down, we'll think of something."

Was she crazy? My plan was to find a cave and hide

in it. As I looked around for one, I noticed a tiny pink flower growing in a bush.

"Sweet sleeping star," I whispered.

"What did you say?" Crimson asked.

"That's a sweet sleeping star bush," I told her. "If you crush the petals and mix them with water into a paste, they can put you to sleep. All you have to do is smear some on your skin, and in five minutes you fall asleep for a whole day."

"Sounds like a plan to me!" Crimson smiled, her calm and steady voice tinged with excitement. Or perhaps it was urgency—she was hard to read. "There's a bridge a mile or two further on. Wouldn't it be good if they fell asleep right into the water?"

"We better get to work," I said, somehow forgetting my fear. Was it the way she smiled at me, as if she was saying this was going to be easy?

Looking in Crimson's saddlebag I found the water

bottle, as well as a small bowl. It never occurred to me then to wonder why everything was there at just the right time, but I was to learn that Crimson was always a few steps ahead of me.

I picked some flowers and mixed them into a paste with a stick, being careful to get none on myself. It didn't take long until I had enough for all ten jogotchies.

Ten jogotchies . . . oh dear. I hadn't thought that part through.

"Crimson, how do you think we'll get this paste onto those jogotchies?" I asked.

"We'll ride past them and you can dab some on their bodies."

"And how will we do that without being caught and turned into jogotchy dinner?"

"Don't worry Malin, we'll go invisible—remember? We'll be safe. Now there's no time to talk. Put on your cloak."

19

Once again, as with the river monster, calmness came upon me and I found myself doing as she said without protest.

"Don't put your hood on until you're on my back. Look in my bag. There's a thin blanket that covers my whole body."

Sure enough, I found it. It was incredibly light and made of a strange white fabric.

"Put it over me, but keep your hand on me," Crimson said. The blanket was designed with a piece to cover Crimson's head and body, even her saddle, and as it slipped over her, she disappeared. I gasped.

"It's all right, I'm still here. Feel my saddle and climb up."

I pulled myself into her saddle, outlining it with my hands first. I wasn't invisible, so it would have looked like I was floating in mid-air—I was so amazed at this thought that I forgot about the jagotchies.

What if I did a handstand on her saddle? Wouldn't that be something to see? I wanted to lie flat and put my arms out and pretend I was flying like a bird, but Crimson started talking, interrupting my thoughts.

"Now, pull on your hood then hold the bowl tight under your cloak. Use the rag that's in the cloak pocket to dip into the bowl. Be careful you don't get any on yourself. Put your hands through the loops just inside the cloak. They will help balance you. Are you ready?"

"Yes," I lied. How could I ever be ready for this? Still, I found the loops in the cloak and did as she asked.

"When we approach the jogotchies, hold your arm out and touch as many as you can with the paste."

With that, she was away. The jogotchies were walking two by two, and I caught my breath as we approached them. They were huge! And the only skin that wasn't covered in thick hair was on the back of their necks. I'd have to stand up on my stirrups to dab the mixture there.

Crimson slowed down and trotted slowly past the first one. I stood up, reached out, and dabbed. Success! Almost. The jogotchy lifted his arm to scratch his neck and nearly entangled me, but I managed to pull away. We approached the next one, and the next one—it was working!

We passed by all five on one side, so now all that was needed was to go around the other side and dab the other five. Crimson rode away from the jogotchies, turning and going behind them, approaching the other side from behind again. The jogotchies were looking out for mosquitoes, thinking they were biting their necks. I would have to dab them with my left hand, which wouldn't be so easy.

As we came up to the first one I had to duck and swerve to get the paste onto his neck. I nearly came off the saddle, but then I felt a strange sensation from the cloak, almost as if it were righting me and keeping me steady. That was good, because the other jogotchies were jumpy and I needed help to keep my balance. Finally, there was only one to go. I stood up, then disaster! He swung around just as I was reaching back from dabbing him and—whack—I fell on the ground at his feet, dazed.

I looked up to see the jagotchy reaching down for me. My hood had come off!

Terror catapulted me into action—I grabbed the dagger from inside the cloak and shoved it in his outstretched hand. He yelped and pulled back.

I pulled on my hood, jumped up and and ran away. The jogotchy was swinging around, trying to find me. I searched around, but of course I couldn't see Crimson. Then I saw a flash a few yards to my right. Crimson. She'd managed to toss her cloak off her head so I could see her—but so could the jogotchies!

I ran and hurled myself on her back, screaming, "Go, go, go!"

She sprung away just as a jogotchy was upon us.

I pushed her hood back over her head and we raced on towards the bridge. Once there, I jumped down, trembling all over. I took Crimson's hood off and then mine.

I'm sure Crimson could see I was shaken, but she didn't give me a chance to complain.

"You were great Malin but now we need to give the jogotchies something to do to keep them on the bridge. Inside your cloak in the lower pocket are two bands. Put them around your wrists. They'll give you the strength to lift those boulders over there in the water up onto the bridge."

I was astounded. I'd never been strong; any child my age at Mastor Ashton's could beat me in arm wrestling. If only I'd had the wrist bands back then. I imagined the boys' reactions to my super strength as I heaved six huge boulders up the side of the bank to block the middle of the bridge.

It didn't take me long to move all the boulders, but we only had just enough time to put our cloaks over our heads before the jogotchies rounded the corner. They were so cross, steam was coming out their ears. When they saw the boulders they became even angrier. They were heaving them off the bridge when the first jogotchy toppled over the edge and fell asleep in the water. It wasn't deep, and he lay with his head resting on a boulder, above the water level.

The other jogotchies looked around, confused, as one by one they all fell down. When the last one slumped over the boulder in the middle of the bridge, Crimson let out a shout of victory.

"Come on, we'll need to hurry if you want to enjoy the birthday celebrations." she said. The idea of a birthday cheered my heart and pushed away the dregs of dread I felt when I looked at the jagotchies.

We rode back to the castle of Sir Alexander, the Duke of Llodorney. He obviously knew Crimson well and was only too pleased that the jogotchies were out of action and sent his men to deal with them. Judging by the swords they took; I don't think the jagotchies were going to ever wake up.

Crimson still didn't want people to know Sir Ivor had retired, so told Sir Alexander that he'd had to leave on other business. I was introduced as Sir Ivor's squire, and was allowed to join in the festivities. The fun and the food were irresistible, especially for a kitchen maid! I made the most of it, especially the apple pies, because I had a feeling there wouldn't be much of this kind of cooking again for a long time.

Chapter 3. The Shadow-Bloods

The next morning we said goodbye to Sir Alexander and rode away, keeping to fields rather than the road as Crimson didn't want anyone to see us. It was a sunny morning and I was ready for a swim when we reached a river.

"Go on then, show me your swimming skills," Crimson said as I slid off her back. I ran into the water, then turned and splashed Crimson as hard as I could.

"Very funny, Malin. Do you want to walk the rest of the way?" she asked.

"No!"

I swam out to the middle of the river. Most girls my age couldn't swim, but my father had thrown me in the water to cool off ever since I was little, so I was at home in the river. The current was slow and it was taking me in the direction we were heading, so I rolled over and lay on my back and let myself drift along.

Crimson was already on the other bank but further behind me when I heard a shout.

"Help! Help my baby!"

I spun over and spotted. . .well, I wasn't sure what it was, but judging by the splashes, it wasn't your average-size baby. It must have been as big as me, and I couldn't tell whether it was a boy or a girl. Perhaps it wasn't even human.

I yelled out to it as I came closer, trying to get it to calm down.

It paused but then went under and didn't surface. I took a deep breath and dove down after it. I could see it beneath me and I stretched out my hand.

Woosh! It grabbed my wrist and I felt myself being pulled down. I was going to drown! Panic seized me and I felt my air escape out my mouth.

Then I remembered the strength bands. I'd been wearing them since the day before, lifting all sorts of things that I wouldn't usually be able to budge. When the cook wasn't looking, I'd moved his largest cauldron full of stew onto a table. He'd had to get two men to help him move back to the fireplace—it'd made him hopping mad!

I wasn't going to drown! I moved my hand so I was holding onto the wrist of whoever had me in their grasp and yanked at their arm, pulling them level with me. Next I grabbed at their clothes with my other hand and starting kicking myself upwards. It felt like I was holding onto a pebble, and we surfaced together then coughed and spluttered in each other's face.

A troll. It looked like a troll! I had to get away, but it clung to me. If I let go, it'd pull me down again. So I turned and swam to the shore, yanking it behind me. I dragged it onto the sand and only then did it let me go.

I jumped up and ran. I would have kept on running except Crimson stepped in front of me and I crashed into her stomach.

"Slow down, Malin," she said.

My words came out in gasps. "It's . . . it's a troll."

"Since when do trolls come out in the middle of the day?" asked Crimson.

I looked at her face, calm and composed, with a flicker of a smile. Relief washed over me and I stood up straight.

"It's a Shadow-blood. They're much more frightening than trolls." Crimson shivered.

A Shadow-blood. They lived in the mountains and were never seen by humans. If you did see one, they would hunt you down and strangle you.

I felt my neck.

"You don't believe that nonsense about being strangled?" asked Crimson.

"But . . . but you said they were scarier than trolls," I said. "And you shivered. Why are you scared if it's not true?"

Crimson laughed and shook her head. "I was pulling your leg, Malin. There's nothing to worry about. Shadow-bloods keep to themselves because people believe the strangling stories and are cruel to them. Come on. Let's go and talk with them. You're quite safe."

I was still facing Crimson, my back to the Shadow-Bloods.

"There's more than one of them?" I whispered.

"Yes, there's the one you rescued, and his mother."

I trembled and leaned my head against Crimson's stomach.

"Do we have to? Can't we just run away?"

"No, we can't," Crimson snorted.

I stood up slowly and turned around. The mother was big as a giant, with a long fat nose, beady eyes peeping out from under saggy skin, and what looked like moss and leaves for hair.

She smiled at me as I approached, and her cracked lips separated to reveal large, jagged, crooked teeth. She took two steps towards me and lifted me in the air and held me to her chest. Instead of being squashed to death, I was held gently, as though she thought I was as fragile as eggshells.

"Thank you," she said, and I felt sticky, snotty tears run down the back of my neck and drip into my hair. Now I really needed a swim.

"You saved Snowdrop's life! You saved my precious son!" she said as she put me back on the ground. I glanced at Snowdrop. He stood up to my shoulder and looked like a miniature version of his mother, except his moss was longer and plaited. His eyes were a lot bigger too—or it could have been that the skin around them wasn't quite so saggy. He certainly didn't look like a Snowdrop. More like a boulder-

breath. He grinned and threw himself at me, knocking me to the ground.

"Ow, let go!"

"Oops, sorry. Mother told me humans are breakable. I just forgot. You were so strong, pulling me up like that."

He looked at me, grinning so much I thought his face might split in two.

"Oh, it was nothing. It's what anyone would do," I said.

"No they wouldn't," said his mother, shaking her head so fast I felt a breeze. "Most humans would have just stood and watched Snowdrop drown. And they would have laughed, too."

I shuffled my feet in the sand. Would I have rescued Snowdrop if I'd known he was a Shadow-blood? I couldn't say.

Crimson looked at me, and I knew she could tell what I was thinking. She smiled at me and then turned to

Snowdrop.

"What were you doing in the water, Snowdrop?" she asked.

"I went in after a slithery, but it wrapped itself around my ankle and was trying to pull me down. But then all of a sudden this boy yanked me so hard, the slithery let go and we popped to the top again."

He waved his arms around and did a jump.

"You're Crimson, aren't you?" asked the mother.

Crimson nodded and Snowdrop dropped his hands and stepped closer to his mother.

"Is it true you stab naughty Shadow-blood's eyes out with your horn?" he asked, almost in a whisper.

Crimson frowned at me when I laughed out loud.

"Of course not," she said.

"Is it true that Shadow-bloods strangle people who stare at them?" I asked.

"Of course not," said Snowdrop, and then grinned. "Is it true that Crimson puts a wart spell on you if you annoy your sister too much?"

Now Crimson frowned at him. "You've got to be kidding," she said.

"Who needs a war horse when you've got a wart unicorn!" I said in-between snorts of laughter.

Crimson frowned at me so hard, I thought I better get control of myself or I would be walking for the next few days.

"Is it true," I asked, turning my attention to Snowdrop again, "that Shadow-bloods sprinkle people's bones on their breakfast?"

"Yes, that's true," Snowdrop said.

I gasped.

"Of course not!" Snowdrop said, clutching his stomach in laughter. "You should have seen your face."

"I knew you were kidding," I said, then tried to

change the subject. "Are you as fast as they say you are?"

"Faster," said Snowdrop. "Want to race?"

"Sure," I said. "Race you to that tree."

"Okay," Snowdrop said, then took off without warning. Shadow-bloods might not be a lot of things, but they were definitely cheats!

We spent the rest of the morning racing and playing. It was a lot of fun, being a kid again. I hadn't had that much fun since before my father died. Crimson sat in the shade and talked with Snowdrop's mother, whose name was Pearl, while Snowdrop and I played hide and seek, climbed trees, and skimmed stones.

I was sad to see them leave after lunch, but they were on their way to visit cousins and wanted to get there before the end of the day. Otherwise they'd have nowhere to stay— no human would ever invite them in.

"You can always stay with me, except right now I don't have a home," I said to Snowdrop.

"Thank you, Malin. Don't forget to come visit me sometime when you're in Milonderland."

Milonderland was one place I didn't want to ever go close to, so I doubted I'd ever get to see Snowdrop again. We rode off, with me turning every few minutes to wave goodbye.

"Shadow-bloods aren't so bad, are they?" asked Crimson.

"Nope, they're fun," I said. "But there is one thing Snowdrop said that has me worried."

"What's that?"

"Is it true that you turn into a big green dragon when no one's looking, and set Shadow-blood's hair on fire?"

The next thing I knew I was tossed onto the ground. I spent half an hour walking behind Crimson before she turned, laughed and then walked beside me, telling me all the funny things she'd ever heard said about unicorns.

Chapter 4. Kolby and the Dwarves

Crimson seemed agitated as we rode on, deeper into the forest. If a river monster or a band of jagotchies hardly drew a look of concern from her, I figured there must be something dreadful on her mind. Something nerve-frying.

"Can't you even give me a clue where we're going?" I asked again.

"Not yet, Malin." Crimson looked around, sniffing the air. "Please be quiet."

We rode on in silence.

I had known Crimson for a few weeks now, but she was still as much a mystery to me as when we first met. I'd explored the cloak and discovered many of its secrets, but was no closer to understanding Crimson. She was magical and mysterious, I told myself, and decided I'd probably never understand her. Better to keep an eye out for dragons than waste time trying to figure her out. She obviously knew where we were going, as she sidestepped fallen logs and broken branches, picking out a track through the undergrowth that I wouldn't be able to trace again even if my life depended on it. Hopefully it wouldn't.

After a while, Crimson halted, sniffed the air then walked over to a wide, tall tree, and told me to hop down.

"Push that little branch above your head to the left," she told me. When I finally found out which branch she meant, I pushed it gently. To my amazement, a crack appeared in the base of the tree.

"Now push the one next to it upwards," Crimson said, tossing her head. As I pushed the branch upwards, the crack deepened and a door appeared in front of us.

"Quick," Crimson said. "We're being followed."

I pushed on the door and it opened silently. Crimson stepped into the tree with me beside her. As the door shut I thought I saw a movement in the bushes behind her but my attention was snatched away by the broad spiraling staircase in front of me. Crimson looked at me and smiled, the tension falling from her face. It must have been the thing that moved in the bushes that was worrying her. Hopefully we were safe now.

"Made it," Crimson said and relaxed. "Follow me." She stepped up onto the staircase and made her way to the top. She paused for a moment and turned her head back to look at me.

"Don't talk too much, and try not to ask any questions," she said.

I reached the top and stepped out onto a platform amongst the branches. From there I could see a whole network of intertwining paths and platforms between the trees. Dwarfs raced to and fro on the other platforms, but it was remarkably quiet for all the bustling that was going on. That must be why I hadn't known they were there when I was on the ground. On our platform a solitary figure leaned against the railings, his back towards us. He must have heard us, because he turned around.

"Crimson. You do realise you've been followed, don't you?" He frowned at her. He was a tall young man, with black hair and dark eyes. I thought he looked striking, but I didn't like the tone he used with Crimson. I took an instant dislike to him and stiffened, placing my hand on the hilt of my dagger that I now wore at my side everywhere I went.

Crimson tossed her head. "I know. I thought your archers would like a different target to practice on for a change," she said with no annoyance in her tone. "How are you, Kolby? Do you like being in charge of all these dwarfs?"

Kolby smiled and relaxed. "It's not so bad. They're a good group. But we really need you to find Juxston. I plan to come with you on your next journey, but I can't leave here until Juxston arrives."

"I can handle the next journey by myself. My boy Malin here can help with any trouble."

41

As Kolby looked me over, I couldn't be sure that he was fooled about my being a boy, especially as his eyes studied me for some time. Then he seemed to hear something. Turning, he shouted out, "Good catch, Faolin!"

Crimson and I moved over to the railing. We could see a couple of dwarfs carrying a vile-looking wolf between them. It was still. Dead still.

"Is it dead?" I asked before I could stop myself, forgetting that Crimson wanted me not to ask any questions.

"No. Just asleep, for now," Kolby said in a grim voice. "One of Taymin's wolves, Crimson. A few more minutes out in the open, and you could've been his next feast. I think you could do with me on your next journey. I do know a few things about hunting the likes of his wolves. And it's not just you who needs protection."

He glanced my way.

"He was never going to attack us," Crimson said. "He's a scouting wolf. He'll be due back at Taymin's in a day or two with news of our whereabouts. I wanted him to follow us here. If you give me some time with him, I'll be able to have him return with completely inaccurate information. In the meantime, perhaps you can have your best instructor teach the boy some things with the bow and arrow. He's making progress, but he's slow to catch on to things."

Now I turned bright red. Crimson and I had been spending our afternoons working on my archery skills. I thought I was doing well, at least until the last lesson when Crimson had introduced moving targets. I hadn't been able to hit a single one.

"All right Crimson, but we'll talk some more later," Kolby said. He stared at Crimson with a frown on his face for a few seconds before turning and yelling out orders in dwarfish language.

Soon Crimson was being shown the way to the wolf, and I was on my way across the trees to the archery master. He spent the afternoon with me, and I improved my accuracy from misses to bull-eyes. It certainly was easier to learn from a dwarf than a unicorn!

I didn't get to see Crimson until later that evening when I joined her for a meal. She was in heated conversation with Kolby when I walked in, but they both fell silent as I approached. "What's the matter?" I asked, looking at Crimson.

She sighed and said, "Your archery skills, son. They're lacking, according to Kolby."

I thought I'd done so well! I felt my face heat up as I blurted out, "How do you know? You weren't even there."

He smiled and turned to Crimson. "See, his tracking skills are weak, too. He had no idea I was watching."

Now I was angry as well as embarrassed, but one stern look from Crimson kept me silent. She sighed then turned to Kolby.

"We've no time to keep arguing, Kolby. Malin and I will leave early tomorrow to find Juxston. I'll give your offer more thought while we're gone. I'll let you know when we return."

"You do that Crimson. But don't take long in bringing Juxston back. We must head off on the next journey within a week or so."

I longed to ask what the next journey was, but I knew Crimson didn't want to tell me. The night festivities went on late so I took myself off to sleep as early as I could, knowing that Crimson's idea of an early start usually meant leaving in the middle of the night.

I was right. We were well on our way out of the forest by daybreak the next morning. Finally alone, walking beside Crimson, I was able to satisfy my curiosity.

"Who is Juxston?" I asked, starting with what I hoped were the easy questions first.

"He is the leader of the dwarfs. He was summoned to an urgent meeting of the Congress of Leaders. He should be back by now. He asked Kolby to watch over his people while he was gone, because Taymin the dwarf-hater has been threatening to attack. It was Kolby who summoned us."

"How?" I asked, surprised.

"Candles in the window at Sir Galvin's Castle as we passed last week," Crimson said.

"I saw those! I thought it was strange to have candles lit there in the middle of the day."

"Next time you see something strange, let me know. It could be important."

It struck me that perhaps I needed to be a bit more aware of what was going on around me.

"Why does Taymin hate the dwarfs?" I asked.

"The feud between his clan of people and the dwarfs has been going on for over a hundred years now. No one knows what started it but Taymin likes to keep it going. His heart is full of bitterness and hate."

He sounded like someone I didn't need to meet in a hurry.

"Where are we going to find this Juxston?" I continued after a brief pause.

"The congress was held at Sir Yearbury's Castle. It's a day's journey from here."

We had come to the edge of the forest, and stepped out of the shelter of the trees into a drizzle. I wrapped the cloak round me and warmth enclosed me. Once on Crimson's back she rode at a steady pace. By the middle of the next morning we were hiding behind some large boulders and looking across fields to Sir Yearbury's castle.

Chapter 5. Taymin's Wolves

"It's too quiet," I said. "There's nobody about."

"Yes there is. Look up there," Crimson said. I peered towards the top of the battlements, where I could make out some dark lurking shapes. They reminded me of something else I'd seen recently.

"Wolves! Are they Taymins?" I asked.

"Of course," Crimson said. "It's just as I suspected. He's tricked the dwarfs. They've put all their efforts into protecting themselves when Taymin only wanted Juxston, their leader. There may not even have been a conference. It was probably nothing more than a ploy to get Juxston by himself."

"Surely he wouldn't have travelled alone?" I asked.

"No. He had a team to protect him. We better get inside and see what's happened to them."

"It's no good going invisible, Crimson. Won't wolves be able to smell us?"

"Good to see you thinking Malin. You're right. But I have another idea." Crimson said.

She sounded determined so I pulled on our hoods and climbed on her back. She crept over to the trees at the edge of the fields, like a sailor stranded on a raft amongst a shiver of sharks. Finally she stopped, and told me to get down and pull off our hoods.

"What you're about to see no other person has ever seen, and you mustn't ever show anyone else. Do you understand?" she asked.

A tingle of excitement raced up my back and I nodded my agreement. Crimson bent down and tried to push aside a sharp bush of brambles that scratched her nose. I wrapped the cloak around my hand and heaved the bush aside. There behind it was a wooden door, only big enough for Crimson to squeeze through.

We pushed the door open and stepped inside to a musty chamber with a tunnel running downhill.

"How come this has never been found?" I asked, my mouth gaping wide.

"Unicorn magic. We made it many years ago to protect our comings and goings. Only unicorns and those we permit can find it."

"How many unicorns were there?"

"Once, there were hundreds of unicorns, all of whom worked to keep the peace and protect people from evil. There are only a few of us left now."

She seemed old and sad then, and I was sorry I'd asked. She smiled at me.

"Come on. There's no time for reminiscing now. Let's go," she said.

We made our way down the tunnel as it twisted and turned. It got a bit slippery as we went under the moat, and then we stepped into a smaller chamber.

"Through that door is the duchess's daugher's wardrobe. When we built the tunnel, the duke and his family worked with us. The current duke and his family don't know about the door—it's invisible from their side. If you ever need to return this way, stand in front of the panel with the unicorn engraved on it and say, "Open, secret unicorn door."

She saw my surprised look—I thought a magical saying would be a much more, well, impressive.

"The original designer of the tunnel wasn't too concerned with fancy-sounding magic words," she said in a dry tone.

It must have been Crimson who had designed the tunnel.

I pushed the door ajar and peered out. Clothes, and fancy ones at that. I pushed aside the gowns and we stepped into the duchess's daughter's spacious wardrobe.

"Bow and arrow," Crimson whispered.

I peered round the corner, where I saw a knee-wobbling landslide-sized wolf creeping up on a terrified lady standing on a bed with a dagger in her hand.

I pulled out my bow and arrow, took aim, and fired. Missed! The wolf turned and moved in our direction. Three bounds, and he'd be on top of us. He couldn't see us but I knew he could smell us. I grabbed another arrow and felt Crimson jump in front of me. Trusting she was there, I leaned on her back, steadied my arm and fired again. The wolf was almost on top of us, and I could see his sharp piercing teeth as I let my arrow go—even I couldn't miss at this short distance. He fell down with a howl, writhed on the floor, and was still. I could see a dagger poking out from his ribs and realised the lady had thrown it. She saved us! I started to tremble, relief washing over me. Looking over to her, I could see she was shaking as well, as she picked up a candle stick and waved it in our direction.

"I'm not afraid of ghosts!" she shouted.

I remembered I still had my cloak on: she couldn't see us. I threw off my hood, pulling Crimson's off at the same time.

"Crimson!" she burst out. "Thank goodness it's you!"

"Lady Rebecca, glad to be of service," Crimson said. "Let me introduce my helper, Malin."

I stepped forward and bowed. She nodded absent-mindedly in my direction, before going on.

"Taymin's wolves are guarding our rooms. This one was supposed to be watching me, but I think he got a bit hungry," she said, shivering again.

"Where is Juxston? Is he alright?" Crimson asked, kicking the wolf aside with her hind legs.

"He's down in the Banquet Hall. Taymin's got him tied up with five wolves guarding him."

"What about your parents?"

"They're being kept in Father's room—down the passageway with two wolves guarding the door."

"Is there anyone else on this floor?"

"No, just us. All the guards and servants were poisoned and locked in the dungeons."

As she spoke, I heard a scream from down the passageway. We raced to the Duke's room. He and the Duchess were being backed into a corner by two growling wolves. I grabbed an arrow and fired at the wolf closest to the couple. Somehow my arrow hit its mark and the wolf fell to the ground, writhing. But the second wolf whirled around and jumped at me.

"Dagger!" I heard Crimson yell but I was already pulling it out. I held it up in front of my face, but the wolf was on top of me, his open mouth filled with savage-looking teeth intent on ripping me to shreds. I thrust the dagger into his neck, protecting my throat with my arm. His teeth wrapped around my arm and bit in, and everything went black.

When I came around, Lady Rebecca was wrapping a bandage round my arm. She smiled at me.

"Welcome back," she said. "That was very brave. You saved my parents."

I smiled and shut my eyes again until I could stop twitching. My arm had puncture marks where the wolf had tried to dig his teeth in, but he'd had no time to do much damage. Though the pain hurt worse than anything I'd known before, I was soon standing up again and listening to Crimson and the Duke discussing how to save Juxston.

He was being held in the Banquet Hall, which was two levels high, with a balcony running around the second level that we could access. Crimson told me to put on the hood of my cloak so I was invisible, and go and spy out the Banquet Hall. Thankfully, she came with me. I was afraid of running into more wolves by myself.

We peered over the balcony down to Banquet Hall. I could see Juxston, a stout, bearded dwarf, bound to a chair by his hands and feet. He was directly under the edge of the balcony. Five wolves surrounded him, licking their lips and drooling. Someone, probably Taymin, was lounging at the banquet table, eating from a tray of cold meat and fruit. He seemed to be enjoying himself, almost gloating over having Juxston bound. Juxston's head hung down, as though he was asleep.

We reported this all back to the Duke, Duchess, and Lady Rebecca.

"He's been poisoned, I think," Crimson said.

"What else did you notice?" Lady Rebecca asked me.

"The doors out were all locked. There seemed to be someone scratching on them, as though there were more wolves outside."

"Taymin probably left his trainee wolves out in the passageway. They're a bit wilder than his trained escorts— even he can't be certain they'll do what he says," Crimson said.

"What if we all rush to the edge of the balcony and shoot the wolves?" Rebecca asked, fingering a bow she'd found in another room.

"Then Taymin will command the wolves in the passageway to come and get us."

"Not if they're locked in the room with Taymin," I said. An idea was forming in my mind. "All we need is some rope and some strength."

It didn't take long to get ready. The balcony ran all the way around the hall, except for one part directly over the doors. One of the items hidden in my cloak was two thin ropes, one with a hook on its end. Crimson had told me they had unicorn magic, meaning they were as strong as a normal sturdy rope and they could attach themselves to whatever I commanded them to. It was pretty simple to hang the one with a hook over the edge of the balcony and have it hook to the latch of the door. I pulled the other end of that rope through the balcony rail and gave it to Lady Rebecca to hold.

She was going to pull on it and open the door when I was ready.

The next part was tricky. I had to throw the second magic rope over Juxston, loop it around him, and pull tight. I'd have only one chance. I tied the other end of the rope around Crimson. The Duke and Duchess held onto it too, ready to pull. I also wore my strength bands, though I wasn't sure they would work, as my arm still ached from the wolf bite.

I crept out to the edge of the balcony, right over where Juxston was bound. The plan was to pull Juxston first, then open the door. But as I was getting ready to throw the rope down, Taymin pointed to the hook on the door.

"What's that?" he shouted and stood up to go to the door.

"Now!" I shouted to Lady Rebecca, dropping the rope over Juxston. It missed—I'd forgotten to give my command to the rope! I pulled it up as quickly as I could. The door sprung open, and in came a couple of wild-looking wolves.

I gathered the rope again and threw it, this time remembering to give the vital command.

"Rope—over the dwarf!" I shouted. The rope obeyed me and fell directly over him. I pulled the loop tight and yelled, "Pull!" just as a wolf from the corridor was about to leap on Juxston.

We all pulled so hard that Juxston was yanked into the air and the wolf landed flat on his stomach, which enraged him. He saw Taymin climbing onto the table, and started for him.

It didn't take long to heave Juxston over the railing. Taymin was fighting off the wolves with a lit torch.

"Throw him the rope, too," Crimson said. I threw the rope again—not forgetting to command it—Taymin grabbed it, and we pulled him up out of harm's way. The trapped wolves started fighting each other in a tornado of teeth and fur.

It didn't take long for Taymin to be bound and Juxston to be freed. We then let the guards loose from the dungeons—they all seemed to wear an embarrassed shade of red on their face. I could see their sense of being in control return as they stood on the balcony and used the wolves for target practice, killing them all. I knew the wolves were dangerous, but I didn't want to watch them die. I left after only the first few had fallen to the arrows.

Juxston was grateful for our help, but was ashamed about walking into Taymin's trap. He was a tough, blustering kind of dwarf, and obviously wasn't used to being made the better of.

"All's well that ends well." Crimson said and laughed. She wouldn't talk to Lady Rebecca about how she came to be in her room.

We left the next day, taking two days to escort Juxston to the edge of his forest. "What about Kolby?"

Juxston asked as Crimson started to say her farewells. "He'll want to go with you."

I looked at Crimson. I didn't like the idea of Kolby joining us, but my near-misses with the bow and arrow made me think it might be good to have someone more experienced join us on this mysterious journey. Crimson wouldn't tell me anything about it, except that I would manage. I didn't feel so confident.

"Yes, Crimson. What about Kolby?" came a voice from high in a tree. Kolby swung down from branch to branch, landing lightly on his feet.

"There you are. I knew you'd be waiting for us. I hope you've got some of my favorite oats in those supplies back there," Crimson said, as if she really had expected Kolby to be waiting for us.

I laughed out loud. If Kolby could teach me to shoot my arrows straight and swing from tree to tree like a monkey, it might not be such a bad journey after all.

Chapter 6. A Spy from Milonderland

Kolby, obviously relieved he didn't have to argue with Crimson, was impatient to get going. He rode Vanquish, a black stallion that Crimson seemed unimpressed with. Mind you, it took a lot to impress Crimson.

Kolby rode ahead, pushing us hard. Crimson didn't mind, and it was pretty easy for me sitting on her back. I'd become accustomed to riding long distances, and I enjoyed being outside, watching the landscape change around me. We passed through the rolling hills belonging to Sir Yearbury's estate, and were headed towards Milonderland, ruled over by the evil Sir Monteith.

My father had told me I should never travel through Milonderland. He had been there many times on business as a horse trainer, but two years ago, when I was ten, he'd made a trip there and never returned. Master Ashton went to search for him, and came back with the news that my father had probably been killed by a band of robbers, but no one had ever found his body.

Master Ashton and his wife allowed me to work in his kitchen, and found a position for Liliana in Lord Hudson's kitchen. They were always kind to me, but I'd felt miserable. I missed my father, all the more because my mother had died when I was six. He'd been a traveller, working with many different people's horses, and I'd spent most of my childhood with him, helping outside with the animals.

Working in the kitchen was hard, tiring, and depressing work for me. I was happy now to be wandering the countryside with Crimson. Somehow I felt I was where I was meant to be, a feeling I hadn't had since my father died. The thought of my father made me feel even more nervous about riding through Milonderland. Unknown evil had befallen him there, and I dreaded entering the area, let alone spending days travelling through it.

Crimson must have sensed my nervousness for she spoke kindly to me, letting me know when we were approaching the border of Milonderland. It was getting dark.

"I'll not spend the night in Milonderland," I said as she paused for a moment under a tree. I hopped off her back and stood still, arms folded across my chest. "I'll go with you through Milonderland during the day, but I'll not shut my eyes in that province."

Thankfully Kolby, taking a signal from Crimson, agreed.

"Right lad," he said. "We'll camp here for the night. Milonderland is only a ten-minute ride from here, but this is still Greenfell. Tomorrow we'll ride hard through Milonderland. We should get to the West Coast in a couple of days. I know somewhere safe to stay tomorrow night, so let's get some rest now."

Relieved, I relaxed and even started humming as we made camp. I tried not to think about tomorrow. After a rough meal, Kolby gave me some training in using the bow and arrow, an exercise which soaked up my thoughts until there was no room for anxiety. It was only when I lay down to sleep that I started to worry again.

I finally fell asleep but was woken in the middle of the night by a snorting, snuffling sound nearby. I sat up in time to see Kolby soothing Vanquish, before slinking out of the camp, leaving Vanquish tied up.

Without thinking, I yanked on my cloak, pulled the hood over my head and followed Kolby, keeping out of sight amongst the trees. He ducked behind a large tree and seemed to disappear. I raced over and was about to rush around the other side of the tree when I heard voices, so I scampered up the tree instead. I watched and listened to Kolby as he spoke with a black-hooded stranger—most likely a dwarf, judging from his height.

"You sure you weren't followed?"

"No," came Kolby's confident reply. "What's the news?"

"M'Lord's changed his plans. He's no longer landing on the Western shore. Says it's too dangerous. Wants you to meet him on the Northern Shore, at Hunsters Bay. Don't go through Milonderland. Snake's got spies everywhere there. Looking for a lass, but they'll slit the throats of any child, just for fun."

"That'll add days to the trip! Is he sure?"

"A couple of young'uns have been wounded and one killed in the last week in Milonderland. Don't go that way."

Shivers ran down my spine. Children killed! But why?

"When shall we meet him?"

"Go through the Elven forest—not around, it'll be quicker. You need to move fast. He'll be at Hunsters Bay in five days. Whatever you do though, keep that lad safe."

And with that the stranger slipped away into the night, disappearing into the dark. Kolby muttered under his breath then made his way back to camp. I ran past him among the trees, somehow getting ahead of him. I just made it back before him and pretended to be asleep as he came past and lay down again.

However sleep eluded me. There was too much to think about. Who was the dwarf Kolby had met? I was the only 'lad' in our group, so the dwarf must have been talking about me. And who was Snake? Why was he after a lass? Now I was glad for the pretense of my being a boy, but I no longer felt as safe as I had before. And who was "M'lord?" It was all too mysterious, and I longed to talk it over with Crimson. It was a long time before I managed to fall into a fitful sleep.

It was still dawn when I woke. I opened my eyes and saw Kolby talking to Crimson. They both looked in my direction, then moved away. I pretended to still be asleep but inside I was angry. Crimson must know of the meeting last night—would she tell me about it?

I couldn't bear it any longer, so I jumped out of my blanket and marched over to Kolby and Crimson.

"What's going on?"

"Nothing," Kolby said.

"Liar," I said. "I followed you last night. I heard everything that dwarf said to you about staying clear of Milonderland."

Crimson looked kind of relieved.

Kolby was furious.

"You shouldn't have been spying on me!" he shouted.

"It's not my fault if your tracking skills are so weak that you had no idea I was nearby!" I said, trying not to smirk.

Crimson laughed and said, "He's learning from you already, Kolby."

Kolby gave us both a dirty look and strode away, muttering under his breath.

"Please tell me what's going on Crimson. I'm really worried."

"There's no need to be concerned," Crimson said. "Everything is under control. It's dangerous times right now to be travelling, which is why I've had contacts to keep us informed of what's going on. The man you saw last night was one of Kolby's friends who travels about, keeping his ear to the ground. It seems it's too risky to travel through Milonderland because of an evil man called Snake. He's keen to capture a young girl who's the daughter of his enemy, Sir Eric. We don't want them to mistake you for her and run you through with an arrow."

"Who's Sir Eric?" I asked.

"He's a noble man who works on behalf of the King to keep peace in our land. He's been keeping a close eye on the King's enemies. The Snake is one of them—he longs to rule himself." Crimson spat on the ground. She obviously loathed the Snake.

Another question came to mind. "Who are we going to meet on the Northern shore?"

Crimson hesitated a second, then replied as I'd already guessed, "Sir Eric."

"Why?"

"Because he needs our help to succeed in his plans for peace. Now that's enough questions."

"No, one more, please!" I asked. "Why is it so important that I come along, and that you keep me safe?"

Crimson rolled her eyes. "You came along by accident, remember. Well, it may be an accident that you're in my care now, but it's dangerous times and we all look out for each other. It's only natural with a man running around attacking children that we'd be worried about keeping you safe. There's no way we would leave you now, so you have to come along. You have no choice."

Chapter 7. The Elves

We were heading away from Milonderland within the hour. I was so glad to be leaving that I sang myself a song my father had taught me. It felt good to know where we were heading, especially as the elves were known for their kindness. Because of this, it seemed strange to me that when we came to the edge of the Elven Forest, Crimson warned us to stay close to each other. More than that, she asked me to walk beside her with my cloak hood on so I wouldn't be seen. We picked out a track amongst the trees rather than using the main path.

As we headed deeper into the forest, it became eerie, with shafts of light piercing through the canopy. It wasn't a thick rooftop so it still was quite light, but it felt mysterious.

Crimson stopped and smelt the air. "Elves," she whispered. "Hide behind that bush until I call you."

I stepped lightly over to the bush she'd nodded at, so as not to leave imprints in the ground. I was just in time.

A band of elves appeared in front of Crimson, their silver bows strung with arrows pointing at Crimson and Kolby. Kolby sheathed his sword at Crimson's command.

"What is the meaning of this, Jasperfield?" Crimson asked the leader. "I have always been allowed free passage through the Forest of the Elves, and now you greet me with drawn bows less than an hour from the border."

Jasperfield lowered his bow and the other elves followed suit. "We are keeping an eye on our borders, Crimson. There are rumors of war. It seems the Snake is gathering his forces. And there has been a stranger, a woman, coming through the forest. She's looking for children and threatening our people with death if we don't surrender any human child to her."

"How is it that she can threaten you in your own home, where you have always ruled?"

72

"She travels with two mungas, the largest I have ever seen. If you see any human child, take care. She may not be far away."

"Thank you for the warning, Jasperfield. We will keep an eye out for this stranger and her mungas. Which direction are you heading next? Perhaps it would be better if we went separate ways and both looked out for her."

"We are on our way to the border from where you came. Why are you travelling through our forest?"

"We are going to the North to check out these war rumors. If they are true, I hope we can rely on the elves to fight with us against the enemy." She stared Jasperfield straight in the eyes.

"Of course. We would be pleased to see the last of the Snake and his allies," Jasperfield said with heartfelt urgency. "But you need to move fast. Let me know your news on your return. Now I'm afraid we must be going. I want to find these mungas and see if we can't kill them before they kill one of us. Would you like one of my elves to escort you through the forest?"

"Thank you for the offer, but no. We will be all right by ourselves. I will look for you when we return this way."

Crimson nodded to Jasperfield, who bowed, then turned and went back the way we had come.

I tumbled out of my hiding place and ran over to Crimson, letting my hood fall down as I did.

"What's a munga?" I asked.

"Like an oversized wolf, but worse. Something Taymin bred. It will tear you limb from limb if it catches you. Keep your hood on, and hop on my back. Mungas can't climb, so if we come across any, get up the nearest tree."

I jumped onto Crimson's back where I usually felt safe, but as I listened to Kolby speak, I only became more frightened.

"It must be one of Taymin's. He was the only one who was breeding mungas."

74

"Taymin is in a deep dark hole, if the dwarves let him live at all," Crimson said. "Even Taymin submits to someone. He cannot have gathered all his resources by himself."

"I always considered Taymin to be alone in his treachery. Who would possibly help him?"

"The Snake of course," Crimson said. "His mungas are some of the foulest creatures alive. If they are the Snake's mungas, there's only a few people who can control them."

I shivered and Crimson fell silent.

We moved quietly through the forest for the next three or four hours. It was mid-afternoon when Crimson halted, sniffing the air.

"Munga," she whispered. "Up that tree, quickly."

I shot off her back and climbed up the tree as fast as I could.

Crimson and Kolby took a few steps forward, then with a loud crashing sound, they disappeared into the ground!

Chapter 8. Idla's Mungas

A trap. They'd fallen into a pit! I was horrified. I was about to call out, but two tower-sized wolf-like creatures dashed out of the trees opposite me and started baying at the edge of the pit. They looked delirious, with wild eyes and frothing mouths. I felt terror cut through my body. It was a feeling I was getting used to, only this time it was Crimson who was in trouble, not me. Somehow that made the feeling worse.

A woman slipped out of the trees and stood at the edge of the pit. The mungas quietened down and sat calmly at her feet. She stared down into the pit.

"Well, well. What have we here?" she hissed. "If it isn't Kolby, the friend of the dwarfs, and Crimson, Sir Eric's spy. This is a fine feast for my boys tonight."

"What are you doing here, Idla?" Crimson asked. There was no fear in Crimson's voice—she sounded almost bored. "You are a long way from home."

"Not that far, Crimson, not that far. My mungas can run fast and could overtake even you. It took but a day or two to reach this forest. Now where is the child travelling with you?"

"I have no child travelling with me, Idla."

"Ah, my sources wouldn't deceive me, Crimson. I know there is a child with you, apparently a boy. But I will decide for myself when I find him. Where is he?"

"You are mistaken."

"Perhaps, but my mungas will soon find him if he's near."

With that, she issued a command to the monsters in a strange language, and they began sniffing the ground. Soon they would be under my tree. I needed to do something, and fast.

I could feel panic rising as the mungas headed my way, so I focused on what I could see of Crimson from my vantage point. She looked calm and in control. I felt her stillness surround me and my panic fled.

I knew what to do.

I reached to my belt and took out the dagger I'd used to kill the river monster the day I first met Crimson. Putting it between my teeth, I pulled out my bow and a few arrows from under my cloak. Kolby had taught me well, and I was sure I could hit both mungas straight in the chest from where I was. If I missed, I would grab the dagger and throw it with all my might.

I pulled back the string on the bow and let my arrow fly—straight to the chest. The munga fell with a yelp and writhed on the ground. I restrung my bow and let another arrow fly into the chest of the second munga.

Idla let out a cry and looked up into the tree, searching for me. Out of the corner of my eye I could see Crimson put her front hooves up on the side of the pit and Kolby ran up her back, his sword drawn. Idla gasped in horror as Kolby came up behind her and slashed her shoulder. She let out a curse and swirled on him, her eyes blazing. Kolby sidestepped as she tried to thrust her sword into his chest.

It gleamed and sparked and I knew it was magic. My panic returned in full force—Kolby was in deadly danger! I threw my knife without pausing to think about where Idla was moving. She stepped aside and the knife only grazed her. She yelped but was so intent on stabbing Kolby she just kept going. I forgot my bow and arrows, deciding instead that if I could jump on her back from above, I might have a chance of stopping her.

I was about to launch myself into the air when a strong hand gripped me like iron bands and set me down on my branch.

"Don't move. Stay there, and keep quiet!" a voice said from beside me.

My panic doubled in intensity—I thought I might explode! I could see no one, but the voice was as commanding as Crimson's.

A woman appeared on the branch beside me. She was old, with long white hair tied back behind her head. Her face was creased with lines and her lips were thin and wide. The most striking thing about her was her clear, piercing, light blue eyes. They looked furious. She stared right at me, as if she could see me, and I made out that she had the same kind of cloak on that I had, but she had pulled back her hood and become visible. She turned her attention to the scene below.

"Idla," she said with a firm voice. "Stop fighting. Throw down your sword."

Idla stopped and turned to look up at the lady. Kolby grabbed Idla's wrist and twisted her sword out of it, then stood with his sword pointed at her back.

"You," she gasped. "You killed my mungas!"

"You are lucky I didn't kill you," the woman beside me said, not correcting Idla about who had killed the mungas. "Kolby, you put your sword down as well. It's not your place to take Idla's life. There are others, like Jasperfield, who would like to talk with her first."

The strange woman climbed down from her perch next to me in the tree. As her feet touched the ground, another group of elves came out of the bushes, all with their bows and arrows pointed at Idla. The leader looked like Jasperfield, only younger—it was easy to see they were brothers.

"Thank you, Guardian, for ridding our forest of the mungas."

"You are welcome, Faelchir. Jasperfield will be pleased to deal with Idla himself if you care to escort her."

Faelchir nodded his agreement.

"Let's get Crimson out of that pit, shall we?" the lady said.

I watched as the elves chopped off a wide branch from a neighboring tree and hung it over the edge of the pit. Crimson stepped nimbly on top of it, quickly reaching level ground. She gave her thanks to her rescuers, then suggested we'd better keep moving.

The old lady spoke to Faelchir next. "I suggest when you return from Jasperfield's that you bury the mungas in this pit Idla had them dig."

She picked up Idla's sword and examined it. "I think I'll keep this. I'll have this back, too," she said, picking up my dagger from the ground. I guessed she was pretending it was hers to keep Idla from knowing someone else had thrown it.

She put my dagger away in her cloak and spoke to Faelchir again. "I will stay with Crimson and Kolby and escort them out. Tell Jasperfield that it would be better if Idla did not return to the Snake for a very long time, if at all."

Faelchir turned and spoke with Crimson, but I couldn't hear what he said. He then turned and led a very subdued Idla away flanked by the members of his team.

Crimson called me down as soon as they were out of sight. I threw off the hood, jumped down from the tree, ran to Crimson and put my arms around her neck.

"Thank goodness you're safe!" I exclaimed.

Crimson smiled. "I was more worried about you than myself."

I looked down at the dead mungas and shuddered.

Kolby pulled out my arrows, wiped them clean, and passed them to me.

"You must have learnt something from the dwarf archery master."

"Ah, so that is where he learned to aim his arrows so well," the old lady said, passing me my dagger then stared at me, studying my face. I stared back, hoping she couldn't read panic in my eyes.

83

"I am the Guardian of the Elven Forest," she said after a long pause. "You can call me Tanglegreen. Well, we better be going."

She turned and was about to step away.

"Wait," I said. "How could you see me in the tree when I was invisible?"

She turned back to look at me. "I see. You have been so busy learning archery and knife throwing, you've missed out on lessons about your cloak. Don't tell me Crimson likes to surprise you with its abilities just as you need them."

She gave Crimson a disapproving glare.

Crimson just smiled and bowed. "I have been waiting for the best teacher to instruct him."

"Is he ready to know these things?" Tanglegreen asked.

"Most things," Crimson said, and I knew I would not find out all the powers of the cloak. But I didn't mind. I was excited to learn anything I could.

84

We talked as we walked, and the stories Tanglegreen told were magical. Each story involved the cloak and I learned so many new things my head was spinning when we reached a clearing.

"We will camp here for the night," Kolby said.

"It's a good spot," Tanglegreen said. "But you and the lad must sleep in the trees. I suggest that one over there."

She pointed at a large spreading tree with many solid-looking branches.

After a quick meal of dried bread and water I went straight to sleep, my cloak wrapped around me in the way Tanglegreen had said to make it as comfortable as any bed. I chose the most uncomfortable looking branch to test it on, and that was what saved me.

Chapter 9. Bobahos

"Sniff all the good-size branches. The child must be asleep on one of them."

I thought I was dreaming, but I realised I was wide awake when I felt my branch jerk. Someone standing on the branch below was holding onto the skinny branch where I was perched.

Luckily, I was snug in my cloak, with it totally wrapped around my head. I knew I was invisible, but now, thanks to Tanglegreen, I knew it was hiding my scent too, as long as both my body and face were totally covered.

I peeked through a tiny gap and saw a tall, skinny, ugly man clinging to my branch. He was directing a miniature monster on the branch above me. It was about the size of a cat, with long hooked dagger-like teeth, horns, reddish-brown fur, a pointed snout and no ears to be seen in the long hair that grew thick as a dwarf's beard.

It must be a bobaho. Tanglegreen had told me of them, but I had laughed. So they were real. Tanglegreen had said they were expert sniffers and very nimble. They could track any creature even in the most difficult to reach places. They used their front two legs like arms, and had strong back legs for jumping from place to place. Once they found their victim, they latched onto them with their hooked teeth and nothing could remove them.

The ugly man's hands were getting closer to me as he shuffled along the branch. He smelled disgusting—he obviously hadn't bathed in weeks. Soon I would have to move, but I knew the bobaho would hear me if I did. I might have time to reach for my knife as I ran away, but the bobaho moved so fast, it was likely I'd miss if I threw it. If I held myself still and used my knife to stab it, the man would overpower me—his fumes were already unsteadying me. Any longer and they'd likely knock me out cold.

The man's hands were only inches away when he was attacked by a coughing fit. Fantastic—he was so loud I could move unheard, although now I had phlegm-filled air to contend with as well. Foul! I stood carefully—now was the time to test the balancing power of the cloak again. As I slipped my arms through the two loops inside, I felt a tingle in my body and an amazing sense of ease swept over me. I stepped over the man's hand and walked along the branch, back to the trunk.

He recovered from his coughing just as I touched the trunk.

"The tracks on the ground say he's in this tree. I'm certain of it. Keep looking," he said to the bobaho. "We'll find him while those others aren't around. Won't Idla be furious when I get the Snake's reward instead of her!"

I searched the area, my eyes darting all around—where were Crimson and Tanglegreen? I thought Kolby had gone to sleep in the tree as well, but I couldn't see him anywhere. Had they all abandoned me?

Now I was moving, I knew the bobaho would soon pick up my scent. I was in trouble with no way out.

The man let out an unexpected yelp of pain, then stood frozen for a second before tumbling to the ground. He had an arrow through his chest. Kolby must be nearby!

Spurred into action, I took out my dagger and threw it at the bobaho, trying to knock it out with the handle to the head. Bad decision—my dagger did hit the bobaho, but only enough to make it mad. It came scuttling along the branches towards me, its teeth dancing at the thought of my flesh.

I heard a shout, "Take off your hood!"

I obeyed and in an instant arrows were whizzing across from another tree and they all hit their mark. The bobaho fell to the ground, with four arrows sticking out of it.

I looked over and spotted Kolby in a nearby tree. He was difficult to make out in his green cloak, all hidden amongst the leaves. A sense of relief smacked into my body in full force—I would have crashed to the ground if it hadn't been for the cloak's balancing power catching me as I stumbled. I recovered my breath and ran across the branches until I was beside Kolby and grabbed his arm.

"Thank you for saving me!"

"Next time take your hood off sooner so I know where you are. When I shot that man, I had to take a gamble that you weren't in the way!"

I could tell he was worried about me. He reddened slightly. "It's not how I like to shoot."

I smiled. "Where do you think the others are?"

"They went to have a talk about things in private. They woke me and put me on guard before they left. They'll be interested to see what we have here. We better stay in this tree until they come back."

We sat on the branch.

"How does it feel to run along the branches like that and not fall off?" Kolby asked.

I knew it was a skill he had acquired from years of practice, so I felt somewhat a cheat, but I couldn't help boasting. "It's the most marvelous feeling I've ever had."

He snorted.

"Of course, I couldn't possibly be as good as you," I said.

"With that cloak, you can do many things better than any expert. But remember, it's the cloak that does it. If you want a skill for yourself, you need to start from the beginning and learn it like the rest of us. Imagine if you had great balance yourself, how much more the cloak would add to what you have."

"I'd be able to fly!" I shouted.

Kolby laughed and said, "Maybe. We'll start with something simpler though, when we get the chance, shall we?"

I looked excited, until he spoke again. "I don't think there will be much time for training of any sort in the next little while, judging by the Snake's activities in the last day or so. Watch yourself, child."

Chapter 10. The Snake's Eyes

Tanglegreen and Crimson were not long in returning. They looked grim when they saw the bodies and heard our story.

"Sounds like one of Idla's retainers," Crimson said.

I wanted to ask more but Crimson went on in an urgent tone. "We must be on our way. Let's put the bodies up the tree, so no wild animal gets them. His friends will find him when they come looking for him."

Soon we were moving through the forest again and by midday we were coming near its edge. Tanglegreen walked with me and asked me about my life. I enjoyed telling her the stories of the things my father, sister and I had done. It all seemed so long ago. It made me miss my sister even more.

"You'll be able to see her again soon, I think," Tanglegreen said.

"Why? Is she nearby?" I asked.

"No, no." She looked flustered, then continued. "All I meant was that it's just another hour until you'll be at the border of the Elven forest, and soon after that you'll meet up with Sir Eric. When you finished with him, perhaps Crimson can you take you back to visit your sister. I must talk with Crimson now."

She left my side to move up next to Crimson, leaving me feeling lonely for my sister and wondering if there was something she wasn't telling me.

We soon reached the edge of the Elven Forest. Tanglegreen seemed sad to say goodbye, and she held me tight in a farewell hug.

"Be careful, and remember all I told you about the cloak."

I was going to miss her. She seemed so motherly to me—or perhaps grandmotherly. But I couldn't imagine a grandmother hiding up a tree. I smiled at that thought as we stepped out of the forest into the sunlight.

"Well, where are we off to next?" I asked Crimson.

"To Hunsters Bay. It should take us three days. If we have no more problems, we'll get there just in time to meet Sir Eric."

"Will I see my sister then?" I asked.

"Perhaps, perhaps," she replied in a distracted way, looking off into the distance and smelling the air.

I looked out to the horizon. There was a small dark fleck in the sky, perhaps rain clouds gathering.

"Do you see what I see?" Crimson called to Kolby, who was some way ahead of us.

"Yes, I do. Quick! Back into the forest!"

He turned Vanquish and cantered back to us.

Crimson headed back into the trees, stopping once she was safely under cover to watch the birds. It was a flock of black ravens, all spread apart, seemingly searching for something. They passed over the forest and continued on, missing us all together.

"Snake's eyes," Crimson said. "We'll have to travel at night, and hope there is no moon."

Kolby sighed and jumped off Vanquish.

"Well, I guess we better get some rest," he said.

Chapter 11. The Dragon of Death

We headed out again that same night. It was eerie,

riding in the dark, watching as shadows crept mysteriously

closer then slipped behind us as we passed. I kept my face

hidden under my hood as I rode on Crimson's back,

nervously aware of how she kept pausing to smell the air.

Three times we were forced to stop and find cover behind a

tree or rocks. Each time the birds flew close, but never over

top of us.

They stopped flying at around midnight. We rode hard

then, galloping as often as we could.

A few times I nearly came off as Crimson jumped

over some unseen fence or other object. It was difficult to

relax; I needed to have my wits about me, as there was no

moon—something for which I was thankful.

Crimson found a small grove of trees next to a cliff shortly before dawn, and we settled down to rest in a small cave in the rocky wall to wait out the day. She was pleased with how much ground we had covered. She told me only one more night and we would be there.

Twice we heard the cawing of the ravens. They sounded frustrated and angry. They flew overhead for the third time, late in the afternoon, and then trouble began.

Crimson, Vanquish and Kolby were all sound asleep at the back of the cave. I was near the entrance, half-asleep with my hood on, invisible to anyone looking in. Some noise outside reached through my mind-doze and shook me awake.

A band of strange-looking creatures was moving—no, hovering—towards the cave. I recognized them as talywren, small child-like changelings that were known to transform into cats or squirrels. I'd always wanted to meet one—I knew they were friendly to humans, but something made me keep quiet as they passed by me and moved into the cave.

The others awoke but it was too late. The leading talywren, taking fright at seeing them there, spoke out a spell and froze them, like statues crafted by a master sculptor. My mouth clamped shut on a frightened gasp but it ricocheted in my head, making it pound. I was relieved to see my friends were still breathing, and my whole body relaxed, the ache in my head disappearing.

The lead talywren moved over to Crimson and inspected her closely. He started speaking in a strange language, so I touched the clasp of my cloak, knowing if I did so I would be able to understand what he was saying.

"These must be the travelers the eagles told us the ravens were looking for. We can't hand them over . . ." I breathed a sigh of relief at that ". . . yet we shouldn't allow them to travel on until we know more about them."

"The war council is in a week, StoneIce," said another talywren. "We should wait and get the advice of all the talywren leaders."

A week! We would miss our meeting!

I groaned.

With that, the whole band of talywrens was looking in my direction, alarmed!

"What was that?" StoneIce asked.

"Be ready," the other talywren said. "It must be child the eagles spoke of. He is invisible!"

They started towards me, hands outstretched, ready to cast a spell.

I rolled across the floor away from them, and stood up, my hood falling off as I did.

"Don't freeze me!" I yelled. "I mean you no harm."

They stopped short, and StoneIce came closer to me.

"Can it be?" he said, looking at my cloak. "You are wearing the cloak of a Guardian. Where did you get it?"

"Crimson gave it to me," I said pointing in her direction, hoping their wands would follow my finger, away from me. No. They kept them aimed towards me.

"So, this is the secretive and elusive Crimson?"

"Yes, and we need to keep moving or we will miss our meeting. It's important," I said. "Please let us go."

"Well, our land is facing strange times, and there is much trickery afoot. How do I know you are not lying?"

"I am not lying. That is Crimson, and we must be on our way," I said as boldly as I could, ever aware of his outstretched hand. He looked at me for a long moment then went and spoke with the other talywren in quiet undertones, so I could not hear.

"You must prove you are worthy to wear the cloak of a Guardian. Then I will know you are not lying," he said to me after he'd finished talking with the others.

"How will I prove that?" I asked.

"By retrieving the Pendant of Peace."

He looked like he assumed I knew what he meant.

My headache was needling my brain again. "I have no idea what you are talking about."

"Well, you should know if that is Crimson and you are a Guardian."

"A Guardian?" I asked. "Crimson hasn't told me about that. I've only known her a short time and you said yourself she is secret and elusive. What is a Guardian?"

StoneIce wavered, reflecting on what I'd said.

"Well, time will tell," he said, "and if you are a Guardian, you will be able to do as I ask. Then Crimson can tell you herself. Come with me."

I followed him outside and he led me to the edge of the grove of trees.

"A long time ago, the leader of the Guardians gifted us the Pendant of Peace to hold in safekeeping. There was no fighting in the land back then but now however, the Snake masses his army for attack. The Dragon of Death, one of Snake's allies, stole the Pendant some weeks ago. He comes out every evening from his cave, clutching it in his claws and taunting us. While he has it, there is no peace to be found and the people of the land are too afraid to rally against the Snake. If you are a true Guardian you can kill the dragon and return the Pendant to us."

Only concern for Crimson and Kolby kept me from laughing out loud. This was too much like the beginning of my adventures. I wanted to say I wasn't the Guardian, just a young peasant, but something inside me didn't quite believe it anymore. Perhaps I was supposed to wear the cloak. Pushing these uncomfortable thoughts aside, I remembered Crimson and her efforts to get to Sir Eric in time. I realised I wanted to meet this Sir Eric, and if dealing with this dragon could do it, I would have to at least try. Surely I could manage with all Tanglegreen had told me and all Kolby had taught me.

I followed StoneIce. We walked in silence for half an hour or more, and dusk was approaching. At the top of a hill StoneIce stopped.

"There it is," he said, pointing straight ahead.

I looked over and shuddered at the sight.

Directly in front of me was a scorched and blackened hill. There was no sign of any plants or greenery at all. Scattered all around were the bones of dead animals, and even a few human skulls. A strong smell of death hung in the air.

This was going to be worse than anything I'd seen before. For one thing, I didn't have Crimson's presence to steady me and calm my fear. All I had was my headache which now had turned from needles to hammers banging behind my eyes.

"How long until he appears?" I asked.

"About twenty minutes."

"I don't understand. Why haven't you just frozen him with a spell like you did with Crimson and Kolby?"

"No one can get close enough to him—he burns us with his fire whenever we get near. We've tried approaching as cats and squirrels, it doesn't matter."

He swept his hand around, taking in the whole mountainside. "See those bones? Many of them were my friends. No one can even retrieve them for burial."

His despair clung to him, like a bobaho with its teeth sunk in so deep no one could ever remove it.

I stared at him, feeling my heart plummet but knowing I had to try something. I needed to move or I would be too terrified to do anything.

"Well, leave it to me and I'll see what I can do." I tried to sound brave when every part of me was screaming out, 'Run Away Fool!'

I pulled on my hood and checked the wind's direction. It was coming from the west of the dragon's lair, so I ran to the east side and rounded the base of the hill. I made my way up the side of the hill towards the lair, clutching my dagger and picking my way through the bones. Every now and then I found another dagger, and I would stop, pick it up and put it in my belt.

It took me fifteen minutes to get to the base of the lair, and I could hear movement inside.

Clambering as fast as I could, I made it to top of the lair just as the dragon's head appeared. It was immense, as big as five normal dragons' heads smooshed into one, and just as ugly, even from above!

He started to nose the air, turning to look up at me. I pulled the cloak over my face to hide my scent. Through a slit I saw the dragon stop sniffing and come out of the cave.

It was now or never.

I placed my dagger between my teeth, pushed my hands through the cloak's balancing loops, and jumped onto his neck. He thundered out a blood-curdling roar and swung his neck wildly, trying to dislodge me, but I was secure thanks to the magic of the cloak. Not so my dragon dagger— it fell out of my teeth and landed on the ground far below me.

The dragon was getting angry and started to rub his neck against the wall of the cave. I reached for another dagger and stuck it into his neck. It didn't seem to affect him at all.

Kolby's words came storming into my mind. 'Go for the eyes'.

I shimmied up his neck and onto the top of his head. With a dagger in both hands I reached down, stabbing them into each of the dragon's eyes, one at a time.

Now he fell down onto his knees with a roar of pain.

I dropped down to the ground and ran for my dragon dagger. He must have heard my footsteps for he opened his mouth to breathe fire onto me.

I ducked down, and was completely enclosed by the cloak as I skidded along the ground. The fiery blast bounced off me, back into the dragon's wounded face.

He screamed out in agony.

I grabbed my dagger, turned and ran to his front, directly under his head. I gathered all my strength and threw myself at his chest, lodging my dagger as deep as I could into his scales. The magic of dagger flowed into the dragon and then he dissolved into the biggest pile of ooze I'd ever seen.

I stepped away and sat down, shaking all over like an endless earthquake.

Chapter 12. Race against the Ravens

As my ears stopped ringing from the noise the dragon had made, I started to hear whoops and shouts from a crowd of people and talywren making their way up the hill. I stood up and ventured into the cave, rank and foul-smelling as it was. Something gleamed against the wall—the pendant! I took it outside and waited for StoneIce, touching the clasp of my cloak as he approached so I could understand him.

"Are you all right?" he asked.

"I'm fine," I said, still trembling. "Just a bit shaken. I have the pendant."

I held up a thick gold chain with a diamond set in a circle of gold. It glowed a little and seemed to give off a clear light. When I handed it to StoneIce the glow flickered and disappeared.

He looked at me strangely, but had no chance to say anything as the shouts of the villagers were getting louder. I had just enough time to ask him to set Crimson and Kolby free before I was picked up and carried away on the shoulders of a couple of strong men.

"I'll go and get them," StoneIce called after me.

I was set down at the head of a group of tables placed outdoors in the center of a nearby village. People were rushing about, filling the table with wonderful-looking food, but I had no appetite. I was overwhelmed by all the people who kept coming up to congratulate me. I just wanted to pull on my hood and disappear, but I knew that would only cause trouble.

Thankfully Crimson arrived, with Kolby leading Vanquish.

I jumped up and ran over to them, relieved that they were all right. Holding onto Crimson's neck, I whispered in her ear, "Can you take me away from all this fuss?"

110

She turned and looked at me, surprised. "This feast is in your honor. These people have lived in fear since the dragon arrived, and you have set them free!"

"I know, but I only did it for you and Kolby. It's embarrassing to have so many people making such a fuss when it was really the coat, the dagger, and the magic which killed the dragon."

"No," said Kolby. "It was you, the coat, the dagger, and the magic. You are all a part of each other. Come and enjoy the celebration. I have not seen such food for months, and I won't run away from it in a hurry!"

He took my hand and led me back to the table, making a point of sitting next to me. I was glad to have his presence, for he dealt with many of the well-wishers on my behalf and after a little while, I was able to eat and enjoy the feast.

Crimson stood on the outskirts of the crowd, talking with StoneIce, and keeping an eye out for the ravens. After a while Kolby and I excused ourselves, and made our way over to them.

"Well done, Guardian," StoneIce's said in greeting.

I smiled and looked at Crimson, my eyebrows raised.

"It will all make sense in a day or two," she said, "but yes, today you have proven your right to be called a Guardian. But it is dark now, and we must keep moving to stay ahead of Snake's ravens. They will have heard the dragon is dead, and will be racing back to inform Snake."

"You must take the Pendant of Peace with you." StoneIce nodded at me.

"No, it belongs to you." I said. Why would he even suggest such a thing?

"We have been holding it in care for the new Guardian. It is your place to take the Pendant of Peace now. If there were more time I would make something of a ceremony of it, but I'm afraid you have to keep moving, as Crimson said."

StoneIce placed the Pendant around my neck. It started glowing as it touched my skin.

"See, the glow shows that it belongs to you." StoneIce smiled and gave a satisfied sigh. "It is good to finally see it where it belongs."

His tone changed as he addressed Crimson and Kolby. "Now you must move. The ravens know you are in the village and are massing to attack. If they capture you, they'll either take you to the Snake, or claw you to death. I don't know which would be worse. I will create a storm to hold them back with a spell, but you must run ahead of it all the way to Hunsters Bay. I have arranged for the sentinel eagles to attack the ravens as you go through Cougar Pass. But you must race to get there first."

"No more apple pie my friend," Crimson said as I climbed on her back.

We said goodbye to StoneIce then trotted away from the village. Kolby found Vanquish nearby and soon we were galloping across the grasslands. I looked behind me and could see the black outline of the approaching ravens. A bank of strong winds and billowing black clouds reached down from the sky and swallowed them up.

"We must ride faster to stay ahead of that," Kolby called. With that we were racing, the storm ever behind us, slowing the ravens so they couldn't reach us.

We galloped for what seemed hours. I had remembered to hook my arms through the balancing loops in my cloak, so I found it easier to stay on Crimson this time. However, I could see Kolby was tiring. I was worried he would misjudge some jump and fall off Vanquish, but he was a much better rider than that. He and Vanquish kept on going, never missing a step.

I thought we would all collapse from exhaustion if we didn't stop soon when a cliff wall loomed up in front of us. We wheeled around to our right, looking for the entrance to Cougar Pass. The raven storm was getting closer and closer.

"Other way!" Kolby shouted, and we spun to our left. The entrance was up ahead, but we wouldn't get there in time. The raven storm was upon us, their claws and beaks tearing the air as they swooped down to attack us.

I felt a surge of anger rise in me. I reached for the Pendant of Peace, and a loud cry against the ravens burst out from somewhere deep inside me. The Pendant glowed bright and flashed a beam of light into the storm. The light seemed to explode as it touched the clouds, and the ravens were pushed back a furlong.

As we raced the final few yards to the Pass, a huge cloud of eagles arose from the cliffs, talons extended in attack. We paused only for a moment or two to watch the fight. The ravens, caught by surprise, were outnumbered and quickly surrounded. The eagles lost no time and showed no mercy as they shredded them to pieces.

"Let's not watch anymore. It will be messy," Crimson said.

"I doubt any of them will make it back to the Snake," Kolby said.

We wound our way through Cougar Pass. Dawn was approaching as Hunsters Bay came into sight.

Soon we would meet Sir Eric. If I was able to stay awake, that is.

Chapter 13. Destiny Confirmed

Wearily we stepped out of the Pass and made our way down a track through the sand dunes to the shore. There was nobody there.

Crimson let out a tired, "We must be early."

I dropped to the ground, ready to sleep where I fell.

"Don't sit there. It's not safe," Kolby said, ever on guard.

"You're right," Crimson said. "Let's wait behind those trees."

We moved to a safer spot, made ourselves comfortable, and I soon fell asleep.

I was dreaming of apple pies turning into ravens and trying to claw at my eyes, when a kind and familiar voice cut through my nightmare.

"Doesn't look much of a Guardian to me."

Could it be? Maybe I was still dreaming. I opened my eyes and stared, unbelieving, at my father's face. My mouth fell open in shock and the next thing I knew I was caught up in his strong arms, being hugged until I could hardly breathe. I was crying so hard, and laughing so much, I couldn't think straight—a loose wheel spinning out of control.

My father, my precious father, who I had believed dead, was right here in front of me!

Crimson appeared beside him and said to me, "May I introduce you to Sir Eric."

"Sir Eric?" I asked, shocked again. "How can that be?"

"Well, it's a long story, my girl," my father said, smiling at me.

"You must tell me now," I said, desperate for an explanation.

"Come on then, let's walk a little, like we used to."

He took my hand and led me down the beach and along the shore.

"Many years ago, this land was ruled by a good King, but he had to leave to tend to other lands and problems elsewhere. He knew he would not be able to return for a long time, so he asked me to come and watch over his interests here. I came here fourteen years ago, and took on the role of a horse trainer, so I could move around without anyone taking notice of me. This way I was able to find out so much more than I could have if I'd come as the nobleman I was."

He paused and looked back at Crimson, a smile on his face.

"Crimson guided me in all my travels so I was able to learn much about this country and who the people of power really were."

"I never met Crimson when I travelled with you," I said.

"Oh no, I mean much earlier, before you were born. It was while I was travelling with Crimson that I met your mother. She already had a child, your sister, but her husband had been killed in battle. We fell in love and I married her. I told Crimson I would be happy to live the life of a horse trainer for the rest of my days with her beside me and Crimson accepted that. She left me and went travelling with Sir Ivor instead."

He shook his head and gave a wry smile."He loved being a hero."

"Yes, I knew of him," I said. "Tell me more."

My father nodded. "Sure, but there's not much more to tell. You came along soon after I married your mother. We had so much fun when you and your sister were smaller. But then your mother became ill and died, and my heart was broken."

He became quiet and stared into the distance with a lost look on his face. I squeezed his hand and he found his way back to me, bringing the sunshine in his smile.

"I had hoped my role of horse trainer would continue until you were grown up. I wanted to give you a childhood free from the cares of nobility. But there has been so much unrest in the land, and I decided I needed to return to the King myself to convince him to gather his forces to fight the Snake. I planned to take you and Liliana with me—"

"Why didn't you?" I asked.

"I found out the Snake had discovered who I was, and there was a price on my head. It was too dangerous to keep you with me. So I spoke to Master Ashton, who also knew my identity, and he agreed to hide you both, keeping you as his kitchen maid, and placing Liliana in the care of his sister at Lord Hudson's castle."

Oh. That made sense. My father kept speaking.

"We spread the story of my death, hoping it would throw the Snake off my tracks, so he would not go after you both. I told Master Ashton you and Liliana must stay as servants, to keep you safe. I asked Crimson to watch over you too. She said she had been from the day you were born."

He paused and I stared at Crimson, my mouth open wide. She smiled and went a little red in the face.

My father coughed and I looked back at him. "It was Crimson's idea to bring you here," he said. "I was reluctant to release you from Master Ashton's safekeeping but she was convinced you needed a chance to prove you were a Guardian, though I'm not sure she was truthful when she told me your journey would be safe. Sometime soon I want to hear of all your adventures on the way."

I was amazed by my father's tale, and a whirlpool of emotions churned though my body. I wanted to ask so many questions but Crimson spoke up and said we must make some decisions quickly. My questions would have to wait.

Kolby, Crimson, father and his constable, a man named Garroway, gathered together to discuss what to do next. I sat close enough so I could hear their conversation.

"We are ready to fight," my father said. "My men are camped a few miles along the shore and are keen to enter into battle."

"I think we could avoid that, Sir Eric," said Crimson. "If we destroy Snake, his forces would scatter at the sight of your men. Your daughter has killed Snake's Dragon of Death, and his Raven Messengers have been destroyed. She has also captured Idla, Snake's ally. We are in a good position to attack, but first we should see if there is an opportunity to avert bloodshed."

My face burned red at the mention of my name. I looked down to the ground as I felt my father's eyes on me.

"Has Kinsey really done these things you talk of?"

"Yes, sire. She is truly worthy to be called the Guardian of the Land," Kolby said.

That was the first time I'd heard what I was supposed to be the Guardian of, and to hear it from Kolby gave me such a sense of pride that I looked my father directly in the eyes.

"Let me help somehow, Father," I said, despite not knowing what I could possibly do.

"It's too dangerous for her," he said. "Better to draw Snake out with a battle."

"Maybe," Garroway said, deep in thought. He turned to Crimson, "What do you think Crimson? You have put Kinsey in some dangerous situations, and thankfully, she is still alive. Do you think she can help with the Snake?"

"She has gone from strength to strength, with each challenge being more difficult than the previous. She is ready to help defeat the Snake," Crimson said.

"Let me think about it." Father frowned. "As for the Snake, my sources tell me that while you were making your way here, he has been gathering his forces as well. He's travelled north through Milonderland and has reached the Londale River on the Northern border with an army of mungas and tworns."

He bent down to draw a map in the sand.

"Jasperfield has gathered the elves and they are ready at the edge of the Elven forest, while the dwarves and men from each shire are gathering to the North and East along the borders of Milonderland. Lord Lincoln's men are already encamped near the battle lines. So we have them surrounded on two sides, with the ocean to the West. However, the Snake himself travels on the Pegasus of Peril, and demands we surrender."

Everyone looked gloomy, even Crimson seemed downcast for a moment.

"What is the Pegasus of Peril?" I asked.

"A Pegasus is a flying horse. They are usually kind and good but this one was captured at birth by the Snake and poisoned until he became the monster he is today. He is full of bitterness and evil magic, and spreads disease and illness to whomever he passes over, killing them within minutes," Garroway said. "He travels in front of Snake's forces and will bring fear into even the bravest of our men. He flies high enough in the air so our arrows cannot reach him."

Crimson and I looked at each other. I could see an idea forming in her mind and I nodded, hoping she didn't want me to tame a river monster then ride on its head to meet the Pegasus.

"The good thing is the Pegasus cannot be on all sides at once." Crimson said, as indomitable as ever. "If Kinsey and I could approach him without being seen, we would have a good chance of defeating him. Now that she has the Pendant of Peace, she can use its power to knock the Pegasus out of the sky, so your archer's arrows can reach him."

That sounded almost doable to me. Best of all, there was no river monster involved. I felt some hope inside of me kicking back at the cloud of gloom hovering in the air.

"How can this be?" my father asked.

"Yes, Father," I said. "On the way here the Pendant knocked back the ravens chasing us. And we'd be invisible to the Pegasus, so we could get really close!"

"I know Crimson says you're ready, but it sounds too dangerous, Kinsey. I don't want to lose you when I've just found you again," my father said, his eyes full of concern.

Garroway was considering me. "My Lord, if we don't defeat this magical Pegasus, he will kill your daughter with disease the same as the rest of us. I think it is the best plan we have. We must fight magic with magic."

My father stood up and walked down to the shore. It seemed an age before he came back to give his answer.

"Are you certain she can do this, Crimson?" he asked.

"Yes, I am," Crimson said without hesitation.

I couldn't look at her, as sudden, looming memories of my failures threw doubts down on top of my hope, trying to squash it.

"Well, we need to move quickly. Let's go," my father commanded.

Chapter 14. The Pegasus of Peril

I don't know what had made me think this would be a good idea. All that talk of my being ready to be a Guardian must have gone to my head. As we stood in front of the combined forces of my father's men, Lord Lincoln's men, Japserfield and his Elves, I felt far from ready for any challenge, let alone the task Crimson was proposing. My father and Kolby were on their horses nearby, ready to ride out behind us. Although we were invisible, it did not stop the fear creeping into my heart as we looked out at a sea of mungas and tworns, gathered against us on the other side of the river.

I'd never seen a tworn before, and now their giant size and their savage dragon-like faces on each of their two heads sent cold shivers up and down my back. Far in the sky, I could see the dark shadow of the Pegasus. I felt powerless, and clung tighter to Crimson.

"Try to stay calm, Kinsey. This is going to turn into a battle any minute. We must act now. Get out your bow and arrows," Crimson said.

As soon as I was ready, Crimson ran out down the battle line, giving me no time to think. At first I was almost panicking, so strong was my fear, but that same sense of peace and power came upon me as Crimson yelled above the raucous din.

"Look at our men and women. They are all good, fine people. Without us, they die today because of the Snake. He is evil and only wants to destroy us."

I glanced at our people before my attention was recaptured by the sea of mungas and tworns. I examined them one at a time—they were the ugliest things I had ever seen. They started to run at us through the river. The deep water churned and splashed, pushing the tworns to the rear, but the nimble mungas were swimming now, making their way closer and closer, each with a person loyal to Snake riding on their back. These men and women were clutching bows and letting off arrows when they could. Somehow Crimson managed to dodge the arrows. In only a few minutes though we would be engulfed by the fast-moving mungas and they would surely knock us to the ground.

"They will kill your father and Kolby as soon as they can unless we defeat the Snake," I heard Crimson say, and I saw the hatred in the eyes of the enemies who were almost upon us. It inspired a surge of fierce emotion within me. I touched the Pendant of Peace and yelled out in a strange language I'd never heard before. A bright light flew out of the Pendant into the sky and all around us. The mungas, people and tworns were physically pushed back a furlong.

I looked up and saw the Pegasus nearly overhead. We would all die if he made it across the river! I reacted without thinking, and called out again. This time I could name the emotion surging through me: pure fury. The pendant flashed a solid beam, pouring its power straight at the Pegasus, who roared then plummeted into the river and thrashed around in the water a hundred yards to our left.

"Quickly, use your lanarkite arrow," Crimson told me.

Tanglegreen had told me the lanarkite arrow was magic when she gave it to me. It had the power to fly direct to heart of any evil being, but would it work on the Pegasus?

I aimed straight for his heart, but as I let the arrow fly, Crimson stumbled as an arrow hit her in her shoulder. My arrow flew too low, and I was sure it would hit the ground.

But no, it seemed to correct itself and headed straight for the Pegasus.

A munga jumped in front of the Pegasus. Now the arrow would hit the munga instead!

I gasped—there was only one lanarkite arrow, and it would be wasted on a munga! I watched in horror as the arrow pierced the munga, then disbelief grabbed hold of me as I heard the Pegasus let out a scream. It toppled back down into the water besides the dead munga. The arrow had gone straight through the munga and into the Pegasus!

He convulsed in the river and then lay still.

"Look out for the Snake," Crimson shouted. The Snake, who had been riding the Pegasus of Peril, had moved aside and was gathering a group of snarling mungas around him, ready to launch an attack. He aimed his arrows in my direction, though he still couldn't see either me or Crimson.

I reached for the Pendant and a broad shaft of light knocked the Snake to the ground, and once again, all the mungas, even those besides the Snake, as well as the people and tworns were pushed back.

The Snake must have seen where the light had come from, because he focused his attention in our direction. He was a tall man with a scarred face, who wore a snakeskin vest and a hissing snake wrapped around his waist. Something about him reminded me of the dragon I had fought and I felt

133

for my dragon knife with one hand while holding the Pendant in the other. The Snake hissed out a command, his voice drenched in anger.

A blaze of dark green, foul-smelling smoke enveloped me, but the Pendant gave off its own white light to protect me. I already had my arms through my balancing loops in my cloak, so I ducked and rolled out of the smoke. The Snake was trying to work out where I was, using his mungas to find my scent.

I darted this way and that, getting closer and closer to him, then came around behind him. There were only seconds before the mungas would be upon me.

I shut my eyes and prepared to plunge my knife into his back, but I couldn't do it!

Killing a man was a lot different to killing a dragon. The Snake turned on me and spoke a magical spell; I knew it was meant to kill me. The Pendant let out a huge blast of light even as the Snake's fog fell on me. There was a loud boom and I thought I would die from the power of it vibrating through me. I staggered back, falling to the ground, my hood coming off. I knew if I didn't die from the shockwave, the mungas would be close enough to tear me to shreds, the same way as the eagles had killed the ravens. I could see three mungas about to jump, saliva drooling, and my familiar enemy, terror, attacked me again.

I closed my eyes, waiting for the pain to shoot through me as they tore at me, but it never came. When I opened my eyes I saw the mungas lying with Kolby's arrows embedded in their shaking bodies.

A loud cheer erupted from my father's men. The Snake was dead! Weakened by the shockwave, he had been unable to use his magic to keep Kolby's and the other men's arrows piercing his body. He lay in the water, blood flowing from at least a dozen arrow wounds all over his body. He looked more like a hedgehog than a snake.

I saw my father and scrambled towards him. He pulled me onto his horse and took me safely out of harm's way.

Chapter 15. The Wait

Once my father was sure I wasn't injured, he wanted
to get back into the battle. I wanted to go and fight too, but
Crimson was wounded from the arrow in her shoulder and
was weak from all the blood she'd lost. There was no way I
could ride her.

As my father turned to leave a shout of joy escaped
his lips—Liliana was approaching us with a group of Elves!
They must have gone to collect her. We held onto each other
for a long while, before father pulled himself away to rejoin
the battle.

Liliana and I watched from a distance. Everywhere we
looked we saw people, elves, and dwarves attacking mungas
and tworns, forcing them back to the sea. Soon there would
be no escape for them—we were going to win!

We watched Kolby and Father, who were right at the

front of the fight, with Kolby firing arrows and Father swinging his ax at the retreating mungas and tworns

Liliana studied my face. All I wanted was to be fighting too, like Father and Kolby.

"Don't be upset about not being able to join the battle. There are plenty of lives we can save here instead. Come on," she said.

We went around bandaging wounds and trying to make the injured more comfortable. We had worked for several hours when I looked up from a man's torn leg and saw Father and Kolby approaching.

"We've defeated them!" Father shouted. "The last tworn has fallen."

"That's wonderful news!" I cheered.

"It is fabulous news indeed," Liliana paused only long enough to give a brief smile before her concern for the wounded took over again. "But we still have work to do. Look at all these suffering people."

Kolby stared at her and seemed unable to look away. She turned her face up, regarding him for a long moment too. She reddened for no reason at all, and went back to what she was doing.

Kolby jolted into action and jumped down to help me with the leg of the man I was trying to bandage. The man was writhing in pain and I appreciated Kolby's firm hand holding him still.

When he was bandaged, Crimson told me to get on her back.

"No, you're injured," I said.

"We need some more of that Sleeping Star bush to help the wounded. And we need Tanglegreen. I know where to find both. It won't hurt me much to take you—you're so light. Liliana will be safe with Kolby."

I glanced over. Liliana was blushing again. Must have been all the excitement of the battle.

It didn't take me long to gather enough Sleeping Star

petals while Crimson fetched Tanglegreen. She came back with us and set to work giving the wounded medicine she made using herbs from the forest that she carried in a large bag. Liliana went with her, and Tanglegreen talked to Liliana the whole time, explaining what she was doing. Kolby was there to help with anything gruesome. I walked about, putting sleeping star paste on the men who were in agony, giving them some relief in sleep. Soon many others joined us in helping the wounded, and when I looked up I saw my father busy bandaging a bleeding arm.

Finally, we rested. It was midnight, and all was quiet. Liliana had fallen asleep with her head on Kolby's shoulder; I was sitting by my father, his arm around me. Crimson was lying near us. I couldn't sleep: there were too many questions racing through my mind. The most important was what would happen now. Of course, I wanted to stay with my father and my sister, but what would happen to Crimson? Would she come with us? I didn't want to leave her, or Kolby. Looking at the smile on Liliana's face as she slept on Kolby's shoulder I had a feeling she wouldn't want to leave him either.

"Lord Monteith sided with the Snake. He and his only sons were killed today in battle." My father was talking to Crimson and Garroway. "I think my men and I should claim his castle for the King and stay there until we are sure we have removed all Snake's allies from Milonderland. His right-hand men, Foulbait and the one they call the Torturer, weren't in the battle today. We need to deal with them and then perhaps we can transform Milonderland into a peaceful shire, rather than a hideout for thieves and murderers."

"That will take a while, my Lord," Crimson said. "There are many places to hide in Milonderland and many who do not want to be found. If you would allow Kinsey and me to help, perhaps we can bring in your plans for peace more quickly."

"She has proven beyond a doubt that she is worthy to be called Guardian," my father said. "But I want her to rest and watch over Liliana while I find out how much trouble we will have in Milonderland. I will know better what has to be done in a few weeks, and where I will most need her help. I will take Garroway and my men to help."

I tried to protest, but my father told me to be quiet and held me tighter. "Liliana needs to rest too, and like you, Kinsey, get use to her new position as a lady. If she is going to live in Milonderland, she also needs to learn how to defend herself."

He looked over at Kolby and Liliana and was quiet for a minute, as if he was considering something. "I am most grateful to you, Kolby. You saved Kinsey from the mungas today by risking your own life. I commend you for being willing to take your duty to the point of death."

"It was not duty my Lord, but brotherly love. I could not bear to see her killed—I would rather the mungas had torn me to shreds."

He spoke with such a passion that Liliana woke and

sat up. I got up from my father, knelt in front of Kolby and hugged him. He joked, "I'm glad you are alive, Little Warrior, but don't think because I care for you I'll be any softer on you when we are training."

I laughed and returned to my Father's side, wondering how I could ever have disliked Kolby.

"It is training that is most in my mind," Father said. "Kolby, as much as I could do with your help in Milonderland, I ask instead that you would guard and protect Kinsey and Liliana while I travel to Lord Monteith's castle. I would like you to train them in self-defence, and I will have someone else teach the girls what is expected of them as ladies."

Despite my protests, it was agreed. Crimson and Kolby stayed with Liliana and I in the Elven forest. Merrivale, Jasperfield's sister, tried to teach us how to act like ladies. She made some progress with Liliana, but I hated the thought of wearing dresses and being stuck inside, so I avoided my lessons as often as I could. Kolby wasn't much of an ally—he would march me straight back to Merrivale and stay to watch for a while, though I noticed he spent most of his time looking at Liliana.

Often Crimson would help me escape. She understood my need to be outside, telling me I was the Guardian of the Land, not some Lady of a Stuffy Castle full of dust and rules. I foresaw a few battles between her and Father, and wondered whose side I'd take. If only Merrivale would teach me diplomacy—that might come in handy.

In the meantime, Crimson and I explored the forest when we could. Liliana, Kolby and Tanglegreen would join us in the afternoon and we would have the kind of lessons I enjoyed. Tanglegreen would coach us on the uses of plants and trees, Kolby would teach us archery and climbing skills, and Crimson would keep a watchful eye over us all.

Father had said he would send for us after two weeks, so I was becoming more and more anxious by the third week with no word from him. I had terrible clawing nightmares about him being in trouble three nights in a row. I usually slept outside with Crimson and she heard my moaning and would try and soothe me, though I could tell she was starting to worry about father too.

One afternoon, as I was high in a tree and Kolby had his arm around Liliana again, trying to steady her bow and help her shoot straight, Crimson called out an urgent warning. Tanglegreen pulled the hood of her cloak over her head and disappeared. Kolby told Liliana to hide but she refused and stood beside Crimson, joining with Kolby in pointing her arrows at the sound of approaching footsteps. From my vantage point I could see who was coming first.

"It's Juxston," I shouted and everyone relaxed. Everyone except Juxston, that is. He saw us and ran towards us, stopping in front of Kolby.

"Sir Eric is captured. It was a trap, and he walked straight into it."

Chapter 16. Saving Sir Eric

Milonderland. Here we were again, standing at the border. This time there was no discussions about entering. I was impatient to rescue my father.

Crimson stopped without warning.

"Let's get going. I must get to my father!" I was almost shouting.

Kolby reached over and put his hand on my shoulder.

"You may be the Guardian of the Land, but you're still a child. You need to be fearful of the evil hiding here, not foolhardy. Do you want us all to be captured like your father?"

He lowered his voice so only I could hear. "If you don't care about your own safety, at least think about Liliana. Do you want anything to happen to her? You need to keep her safe. If you lose your father, she's the only family you have."

"He's right," Crimson said.

They both believed my father could die!

Their expressions told me I needed to calm down and listen—I had been nothing but loud and fast since Juxston had told us the news. Now, here at the border, it was time to think. And listen.

"We do need to get to the castle as quickly as we can," Juxston said. "There's been talk of a public hanging of Sir Eric. I only hope we're not too late."

My throat went dry.

"Let's travel together, but Crimson and Kinsey need to travel unseen. People will be on the lookout for them. You both need to put on your cloaks to go invisible, then follow behind us," Kolby said.

Liliana gasped as I pulled the cloak over my head and disappeared. I helped Crimson put on her cloak and she vanished as well.

Liliana gasped again.

"You'll get used to it," Kolby said.

"I don't think so," she said. "Let's get going, shall we?"

*****

We were almost at the castle when it happened.

Kolby, Juxston and Liliana were not far ahead of us when the trees on the side of the road moved and surrounded them without warning. Shadow-Bloods! And these didn't look friendly like Pearl and Snowdrop had. They seemed ready to strangle all our friends.

Ambush! And we'd walked right into it! These Shadow-Bloods looked just like trees until they moved. Then they looked like fearsome, bloodthirsty trolls.

148

My legs squeezed Crimson tighter as I reached for my bow.

"It won't work," she whispered. "Your arrows will just bounce off them, even from this close. Looks like they're going to take them somewhere. We should follow. Quietly."

*****

We followed at a distance as our friends were led to a clearing in the forest. At the far end of the clearing was a group of four or five Shadow-Bloods.

"What have we here?" asked the tallest one.

"We found these humans heading to the castle," the ugliest Shadow-Blood said. He was short and thick, with moss and twigs growing all over his arms, and a mass of dark green leaves growing out of his head.

"Who are you?" the tall one asked.

Nobody answered.

"They don't look like Foulbait's usual followers," Ugly said. "Maybe I could strangle the girl. That'll get them to talk."

He shuffled towards Lilianna.

"Don't be ridiculous, Squat," the tall one said. "We stopped strangling humans years ago. They're only just beginning to trust us. Let's not help Foulbait make us out to be murderers. It's going to take us years to undo the damage the Snake has done as it is."

I sat up straight on Crimson.

Kolby snapped to attention too. "You're opposed to Snake?" he asked.

The tall Shadow-Blood stared at him. "What if I am?"

Juxston stomped his foot. "Snake is dead," he said. "He died in battle. And if you're on his side, we'll kill you too."

Kolby reached over and stopped Juxston from pulling out his sword. I saw him mouth the word, "Patience".

"Well, well, SkyBranch," Squat, the ugly one, said. "Like I thought, they're not from around here. They could be useful."

"Let's not be too hasty," SkyBranch said. He strode over to Juxston, took his sword and bent it in half, then lifted him by the front of his tunic so he was dangling in the air.

"Tell me who you are," he said.

Juxston frowned. "If you insist," he said, glancing at the ground a long way beneath him. "We're companions to Sir Eric, and we've come to rescue him from Foulbait."

Kolby groaned and shook his head.

I shook my head in unison. Why couldn't Juxston just keep quiet? He was such a . . . such a . . . such a dwarf! All bluster, no brains.

SkyBranch dropped Juxston and took a step back.

"Well, well, that is good news. If it's true," he said.

He turned towards the Shadow-Bloods to his left.

"What do you say, Pearl?"

I couldn't believe it! Pearl, Snowdrop's mother, stepped out from behind a large Shadow-Blood.

I would never forget that long, fat nose and how it had dripped snot down my back. I shouted her name.

"Be quiet," Crimson said, but it was too late. She must have thought I was just as brainless as Juxston when I pulled off my hood, jumped off her back and ran into the clearing.

"Malin!" Pearl shouted and picked me up so she could stare at me face-to-face. "What are you doing here?"

The affectionate way Pearl was looking at me made me think it was okay to take a risk. "I'm with them. Sir Eric is my father, and we've come to rescue him."

Kolby let out another groan and stared at the sky. "I am surrounded by impulsive half-wits!"

"Don't worry, Ranger," Pearl said with a frown. "Malin is safe with us, and seeing as you're his companion, you are too. But I wouldn't call anyone 'half-wit' if you want to stay safe."

Pearl put me down. "Where is Crimson?" she asked.

Crimson stepped out of the trees, her hood tossed off her head so she was visible again.

"I'm right here, Pearl. It's good to see a friendly face," she said.

"We are all friends, aren't we?" said Pearl, looking around at the other Shadow-Bloods. Her thick cracked lips were pressed firmly together, though one tooth poked its jagged head out between them.

Squat placed his branch arms where his hips would have been if he'd been a person.

"You know these humans?" Skybranch asked, his mouth wide open.

"Yes, Malin here is the one who saved Snowdrop from drowning."

That surprised them. They were all excited, all at once. Even Squat smiled and took a step forward to shake my hand. My whole arm was wrenched up and down so hard I thought it might break.

"Is it true, Sir Eric is your father?" Pearl asked.

"Yes it is," I said.

"Well, well, we must move quickly. The hanging is in two hours. We need to move now. We'll figure out a plan on the way," Pearl said.

One by one we were picked up by different Shadow-Bloods and put on their shoulders, me on Pearl's. Crimson followed beside us.

Pearl's moss-hair tickled my nose so much I sneezed.

"Don't put snot down my neck, Malin," she said.

*****

Kolby, Juxston, Liliana and I were separated in the crowd, watching and waiting. Any minute they'd bring out my father. I felt my palms sweat.

The crowd chanted for my father's death. It made me

want to knock them all over with my pendant, which was burning on my skin, but something stopped me. Something was wrong.

Kolby passed me, bent down and fiddled with his boots, then spoke without looking at me.

"The crowd seem nervous. As if they're scared," he said and then moved on.

That was it. That was what was holding my anger at bay. I looked around again. There was murmuring amongst the crowd, and I felt their sense of unease creep over me.

Guards encircled the crowd, weapons at their sides. They looked ready to use them.

I walked over so I was standing in front of a cart in the middle of the crowd. I knew Kolby would be on the opposite side of the gallows, but I couldn't see him. Juxston was near the commander of the guards by the gate.

Then I saw him—my father. Being pushed towards the gallows, his face beaten, his clothes ragged, but his eyes proud. He stood tall, undaunted.

Someone got up on the gallows platform and quietened the crowd. From Pearl's description, it was Foulbait, Snake's right-hand man. He was a short, skinny man, with grey, greasy hair to match his grey darting eyes.

"We're here today to dispatch with our enemy, Eric the Murderer. He came here to cause war and treachery but we have defeated him!" Foulbait shouted.

Lies, all lies. I felt the pendant flare against my skin.

"With his death, I proclaim to our enemies that I am the rightful ruler of Milonderland and they should leave us alone!"

Milonderland had always been under the King's domain. How could he declare himself ruler? It was treason! Was no one going to stand up against him?

"No, you can't! You are not our ruler!" yelled a man near me.

The next minute he was bound and gagged by a guard

and hurled up onto the platform.

"You'll die with Eric the Murderer," Foulbait said with a grin. "Hang another rope!"

I heard a woman cry out, but had no time to look for her voice, for the next moment a loud crashing sound was heard as the Shadow-Bloods charged through the gate, pushing the bricks out of place so the wall crumbled behind them. The noise was deafening.

I jumped on the cart, and pulled out my bow and arrow from beneath my cloak. Oh, no! I wasn't tall enough to shoot above the panicking crowd!

I looked around and spotted Juxston fighting three guards single-handedly. Liliana was shooting arrows at guards from behind the safety of another cart. Where was Kolby?

When I turned back to look at the gallows, I saw Foulbait staggering from an arrow in his chest. Kolby! Of course he wouldn't miss. He'd shot Foulbait!

Crimson was suddenly beside me. "Let's go get your father, shall we?"

"I thought you'd never come!" I said as I jumped on her back.

"Always in a hurry Guardian, always in a hurry," Crimson said, and then she ducked out of the crowd and cantered around the edges before pushing her way to the gallows.

Squat got there at the same time and stood in between Crimson and the crowd.

I jumped up and cut the ropes on my father's hands, as well as those of the stranger who'd stood up for him. He thanked me and disappeared into the crowd.

"Kinsey, we need to stop the guards attacking the people," my father said, looking around at the people fighting as he rubbed his wrists where the ropes had been.

"Let's go then," I said. "You ride on Crimson. Squat will carry me."

We pushed our way back though the crowd, trying to get to Juxston. Guards barricaded the gate and the hole in the wall, weapons drawn.

"Do you want me to deal with them, Malin?" Squat asked.

My pendant flared against my skin again.

"No, let me." I reached up and touched the pendant. The blast hurled them backwards through the hole in the wall, landing them fifty yards away.

Everyone, the whole crowd, stopped moving and fell silent. A stranger ran out and bent over one particular guard, checking him for breath.

"He's dead!" he yelled back.

With that, a cheer erupted from the crowd!

"The Torturer is dead," I heard people say over and over. Even some of the guards lowered their weapons and shouted with the crowd.

I'd killed him. I hadn't meant to. The people were

happy—he was obviously the worst enemy of them all. I remembered my father mentioning his name.

But I'd killed him. I'd never killed anyone, not even the Snake. I was stunned.

"It wasn't you," said Crimson, standing beside me again. "It's the pendant—it reads hearts. It knew he was evil through and through. None of the other guards will be dead."

How did she always know what I was thinking?

"Thank you," I said.

"Well done Kinsey," my father said, and put his arm around my shoulder. I turned and held onto him, so relieved he was safe that I almost burst into tears.

*****

We rested with the Shadow-Bloods just outside the city wall so as not to frighten the townsfolk with their presence. Father was overjoyed to see us all, and we took plenty of time to listen to his story. He'd been beaten by the Torturer, and in the end I was glad the Torturer had been killed. Apparently he'd been the main cause of the people's fear, forcing their obedience to the Snake and Foulbait.

It wasn't long before Father was strong enough to talk to the townsfolk. They were so thankful that Foulbait and the Torturer were gone, that they asked my father to stay and help bring Milonderland back to peaceful rule.

He was only too happy to do this, so we all moved into the castle and started to make a new life for ourselves. Kolby made a home for himself in the nearby forest, but spent most of his days in the castle grounds, supposedly keeping an eye on me. However, his eyes spent most of their time looking at Liliana.

Crimson promised to be nearby, and she was. Especially when I could no longer bear the new life of a nobleman's daughter. She always knew when I needed to get away. And she loved to throw me in danger's way.

But that's another story. . .

The End.

Thank You For Reading!

Dear Reader

I hope you enjoyed *The Adventures of Crimson and the Guardian* and journeying with Kinsey and Crimson. If you liked the story…and if you'd be willing to spare just two or three minutes…would you please share your review of the book on Amazon (if you haven't done so already)? If you did, it would mean the world to me! Here's a link to my author page: www.amazon.com/author/karencossey. Just type this link in your browser to go to my author's page, and then select *The Adventures of Crimson and the Guardian*. Scroll down to the Customer Reviews section and click on the button "Write A Customer Review" and you'll be taken to a page where you can share your thoughts.

If you like mystery as well as fantasy, you may enjoy my series for 9-12 year olds: The Crime Stopper Kid's Mysteries. Try out the Prequel: 'The Runaway Rescue' for free and see if it's something you'd enjoy. You can stay in the loop about my future book releases and get your digital version for free when you join my newsletter at: www.KarenCossey.com/Newsletter/.

As an author, I love creating stories that you will enjoy reading and make you want to read more. So please tell me what you liked, what you loved, even what you hated. I'd love to hear from you. You can write me at: karen.cossey@gmail.com, visit me on the web at www.karencossey.com, find me on Instagram @KarenCosseyWriter or like me on facebook here: www.facebook.com/KarenCosseyAuthor. Plus I enjoy making book pins about my stories for Pinterest at KarenCosseyAuthor (I could get lost on there for hours!).

Thanks so much for reading *The Adventures of Crimson and the Guardian* and for spending time with Crimson and Kinsey. Until we meet in the next book...

Happy Reading,

Karen Cossey.

Acknowledgements

First and foremost, I want to thank my family for encouraging me to keep writing this story, particularly my husband, who much prefers mathematics to magic. Thank you for believing in me, and for attempting to understand unicorns.

Iola, thank you for your excellent editing of my story. Your critique and guidance were insightful and helpful.

And finally, a big shout out goes to my friend Marion, whose support, encouragement, and proofing skills were a real blessing. Thank you so much.

FREE DIGITAL BOOK:
The Crime Stopper Kids Mysteries Prequel

The Runaway Rescue
The Mystery of the Deadly Secret
For 9-13-year-olds

When Cole and Poet's father is killed, they are left with no one to take care of them. Fearing separation by Social Services, a desperate eleven-year-old Cole runs away with his seven-year old sister Lauren. With nowhere to turn they take a chance on a stranger's help, but when danger comes knocking at the stranger's door, Cole wonders if he'll ever be safe again. How far will he have to run this time to protect himself and Lauren?

Receive the whole story (in digital format)
FOR FREE
when you sign up to Karen's newsletter at:
www.KarenCossey.com/Newsletter/

The Adventures of Crimson and the Guardian

Book One of the Crime Stopper Kids Mysteries

The Trespasser's Unexpected Adventure
The Mystery of the Shipwreck Pirates Gold
For 9-13-year-olds

Logan had no idea that trespassing could lead to so much
trouble. All he wanted was to explore some out-of-bounds
caves by himself but instead he finds a new friend
and a load of danger.
Before he knows it, his new friend and he are captured by
gold smugglers and left in a burning fire!
How will they survive?
And how will they save their friends?

Find out more at: http://viewbook.at/amazonstores

Book Two of the Crime Stopper Kids Mysteries

The Con Artist's Takeover
The Mystery of the Unco-Nerdo School Teacher
For 9-13-year-olds

Meeka has a secret that scares her into silence,
a burden she can't even trust with her friends.
All Logan, Nate and Poet want to do is help her,
but when they uncover a crime,
Meeka acts like she wishes they weren't there.
Will they have enough loyalty and bravery
to not only solve the mystery
but save their friendship…and their lives?

Find out more at http://viewbook.at/amazonbookshop

FREE BOOK:
Cinderella Sarah—Short Stories for Kids

Bedtime Stories for Children, Fun Classroom Read Alouds
and Short Stories For Kids.
For 4-8-year-olds

Find all sorts of fun read aloud children's stories and heart-warming bedtime stories for kids ages 4-8. There are fairy tale characters, pets, school friends, angels, dinosaurs, monsters, and dragons! It's one of those fun books for kids you'll enjoy as much as your child or student!

Receive the whole story collection in digital format
FOR FREE
when you sign up to Karen's newsletter at:
www.KarenCossey.com/Newsletter/

Made in the USA
Columbia, SC
04 August 2020